Grand Central Station

Some Relationships Are Just Meant to Be

MARSHA CASPER COOK

ISBN: 978-1-60414-898-5

Library of Congress Control Number: 2016931588

Cover design by Fideli Publishing, Inc.

PRINTED IN THE UNITED STATES OF AMERICA

Acknowledgements

Thank you to all my friends and family for always being there for me and a very special thank you to my Editor Jeff Fleischer and to Robin from Fideli Publishing, thank you for all your help.

*"All you need is love.
But a little chocolate now and then
doesn't hurt."*

— Charles Schultz

Chapter One

It was one of the first serious snowfalls of the season, definitely not a night for a book signing. Doctor Jack Winston had been warned by others not to expect a crowd, but he still hoped for one. Born and raised in Chicago, he should have known better.

After peeking inside the Maxwell Meyers bookstore and realizing the truth, Jack decided to walk around the block. He had felt very lucky to be able to talk about his book at one of Chicago's finest bookstores. If an author had a successful signing at Maxwell Meyers, the book had a great chance of making it to the bestseller list.

Jack quickly realized that he wasn't about to break any sales records. Hopefully, his publicist would cut him some slack; after all, she had planned the event. Jack might have learned a valuable lesson about mixing business with pleasure, and that sleeping with a publicist wasn't always the quickest way to fame.

He would remember that when his numbers came out, and then he would fire her. He had planned to change his ways when he got married, but so far the right woman hadn't crossed his path. Or if she did, he hadn't noticed.

As he walked around, Jack was having a hard time believing there were so few cars on the Magnificent Mile. Michigan Avenue was so quiet he could hear himself think; it was so different from the usual hustle and bustle. Restaurants were closing early, as were some of the other businesses. Jack didn't like it when his ego was compromised, but it did make him realize he wasn't special, and maybe he needed that. He doubted he would ever forget that night, and decided to learn from the evening rather than analyze it.

All the time he was walking, he thought that maybe it would stop snowing and the night might turn out well. So after three Starbucks coffees, two muffins, and a chocolate bar, he decided to walk back to the bookstore and live with the consequences.

He knew Agnes Blackwell, the manager of Maxwell Meyers, and how hard she worked. He hated to disappoint her, because she was one of the first moms to read his book and actually follow his advice.

Agnes was in the back when he went inside, but motioned for him to join her. She was a little bitty thing, not quite five feet tall, a little overweight, and with very bad vision. Jack could tell by the thickness of her glasses. She had curly red hair and a friendly smile, and happened to be munching on Cheetos, one of Jack's favorite snacks. Agnes offered him some, and he took a handful to be polite. He wasn't really hungry after all of the coffee and chocolate. Jack laughed to himself, thinking that five minutes ago, the last thing he would have thought about was sitting in the office at Maxwell Meyers, consuming Cheetos with Agnes Blackwell.

"Good thing the signing isn't tonight," Agnes said. "We'd be shit out of luck. I've never seen it so quiet. This night is a record-setting one for us, and not in a positive way. Haven't had a customer in hours. Anyway, what are you doing out on a night like this? It's so damn lousy out there."

Jack took a deep breath, not wanting to admit he had the wrong date. He knew he had better try harder not to make mistakes like this, because he didn't exactly enjoy looking foolish. "I'm meeting someone for dinner at Gibson's, and just thought I'd say hello and see how your son is doing."

"Jack, you're so sweet. Sit down and let me show you his progress." Agnes yanked her shoulder bag out of her desk drawer. "Look at his report card. I printed it out."

"Now this is terrific. I'm so glad. Were you able to get his teacher to give him another shot before she switched him to a different class?"

"Yep, you bet. I can't tell you how happy my husband was. We kept trying and trying, but it wasn't until I read your book that it all became clear."

"Good to hear. Save that remark for my signing."

"Damn right I will. And it's okay. I know you thought the signing was tonight." She laughed. "Am I right, Doc?"

He reached for another handful of Cheetos. "Agnes, my dear, you're absolutely right. I'll try not to make this mistake again. So much for my high-priced PR firm."

Jack did have his book signing a week later for *Let's Start with Homework,* and it wasn't great, certainly not up to his expectations. A handful of people were in the store because Agnes promised them free books if they would sit and listen, but they didn't. They were whispering, texting, or on their phones. One thing was certain; they weren't there for him. Jack tried his best to hold their attention, but he couldn't. He promised himself he would never let that happen again.

Chapter Two

(TWO YEARS LATER)

Breakfast was not a pretty picture at the Feingold house. There was always so much going on that it could be very difficult to concentrate. Victoria Feingold sometimes referred to her household as "Grand Central Station," because people were coming and going at all hours of the day.

Despite the chaos, Victoria Feingold had a method to all the ongoing madness. She tried her best to ignore the noise, which was pretty easy for her because she was a pediatrician, and her office was loaded with crying kids all day long. Along with the crying came tantrums and vomiting. Her patients were scared, but she was a necessary evil for them; healthy children were her specialty.

So when everyone in her house was a little off the wall, she just did what she had to do, ignoring all the commotion. That meant calling her service to see who needed her. If all was clear, she could sit down and have breakfast with her kids. If not, she was out the door, leaving her mother to handle everything.

Being both a doctor and a single mother of three was quite difficult. She always hated the word "breadwinner," but that's what she was. She brought home the bacon—not exactly a Jewish expression.

Not only did she have Allyson, Andrew, and Noah to raise, but she had an ex-husband who simply hadn't grown up enough to handle responsibility. Her mother and her sister also lived with her. And, of course, what house was complete without a dog? Angus was not just any dog. He was a schnauzer with opinions, some of which he shared with humans.

To Victoria, Angus was a confidant; she thought he was the only one who really understood her. Victoria and her ex, Michael, were the only two with whom Angus shared his love of the English language. Victoria acknowledged that if others found out, they might be inclined to call her insane.

Because she spent most of her day answering questions from nervous mothers and fathers trying to do the right thing, she sometimes questioned her own ability. However, her parting comment to parents before they left her office was always, "Love your children. Children need love, and once they feel your love, the rest just comes with the territory." One of her college professors had shared those words of advice with her, and she felt obligated to pass them on. She knew they were right.

Her mother, Grace, did a lot of the hard work. Grace was good at it. Obviously, she knew how, because she raised Victoria and her sister, Ava. Well, Ava was another story; she was almost forty and still growing up. She and Michael had similar issues, which caused Victoria to fight with them pretty much all of the time. Before Victoria's divorce from Michael, they all lived a very frugal life due to Michael's gambling problem. That hadn't been fun, but things were on the way up. Victoria could breathe again.

Grace loved to cook, and believed breakfast was the most important meal of the day. Every morning, she served a buffet of cereal, toast, pancakes, oatmeal, waffles, cream cheese, and bagels, just in case someone was hungry. Andrew usually ate more than the others. Grace loved that about him. What Jewish grandmother wouldn't?

The neighborhood had quite a large community of grandparents helping their children live the American dream. After the kids went to school, Grace's friends from down the block would join her to play cards and eat leftovers. They didn't play for money, because most of them didn't have much.

Grace really enjoyed having her friends there, even when she just invited them over for coffee and donuts. She always believed that paying things forward was the way to go.

Noah and Allyson ran in and grabbed juice boxes and cookies. Grace removed the cookies from their hands and replaced them with whole-wheat toast, saying, "You'll feel better if you eat better."

Noah put the toast down, grabbed a bagel, and waited impatiently for his sister.

"This sucks," Allyson mumbled as she loaded up on jelly, making the toast a little soggy and lopsided.

"This sucks," Andrew repeated loudly, and then laughed. He was great at mimicking his older sister, who usually had a comment or two about everything.

The morning network news was blasting in the background. The broadcaster was Simon Barret, a young, good-looking guy. Grace loved watching him. "Quiet everyone," she said. "It's Simon."

"Guess who's at Maxwell Meyers bookstore?" the anchor said. "It's Dr. Jack Winston, the child psychiatrist who has become a publishing phenomenon, with three bestsellers in just two years. People are already waiting in line to have him sign it."

It was noisy in the background, and Grace was a little cranky when she couldn't hear the whereabouts of her favorite author. She would have gone to the bookstore, but she had responsibilities and had to live vicariously by watching TV. "Quiet, everyone. Let me hear this. It will be over in a minute." Simon continued talking and Grace, as always, listened to his every word.

Ava entered, wearing rollers and a sloppy robe, topping it off with a toothbrush in the corner of her mouth. "Oh shit, it's the one and only Simon Barret. Quiet in the house."

Andrew laughed. He always laughed at his aunt because, in his six-year-old world, he found her funny. Actually, Grace wanted to laugh, but she was supposed to be the voice of reason. "Shh…" she said, turning up the sound.

Simon continued, "Jack Winston was born and raised here, so this was where he wanted to launch his book, and he'll be at Maxwell Meyers at noon."

Victoria shut off the TV, never hearing a word of what was said. "Okay, who wants a ride?"

. . .

Michigan Avenue was beautiful during the summer. There were so many things happening on the street. Mimes were performing, hot dogs were cooking, newsstands were busy, and shoppers were sightseeing. Everyone was happy, and very thankful that summer had finally come. Chicagoans knew how short summer was, and they never disappointed Michigan Avenue by not showing up. They came in droves.

Jack Winston and his publicist picked July to showcase his new book. *It's Easier than It Looks* was a parents' guide to getting results, and it was going to be on the *New York Times* bestseller list. Jack's book had the market buzzing, and his sales had already exceeded the publisher's expectations.

Parents, teachers, and grandparents were following his suggestions, with exciting results. Even though he had no children of his own, he had the pulse on how to raise them. His mother was always extremely proud of what her son was doing, and hoped he would be a parent one day—but that was not part of his plan.

There was a crowd waiting in front of the Maxwell Meyers bookstore when Jack's shiny, black limo pulled up. His driver, Morgan, was wondering how his boss would handle the crowd. He watched closely in the mirror while Jack prepared himself by taking several long breaths.

Before he became a celebrity author, Jack had always hated crowds. He certainly never thought he would be a household name, and the fact that he had become one still shocked him.

He had to learn how to publicly express his thoughts, but being personable wasn't hard for him. He was charming and always knew the right thing to say. His smile was as genuine as the love his fans had for him.

Jack remembered his first signing, and that awful feeling when no one was listening kept him very humble. He hadn't seen Agnes Blackwell for a long time, but he always remembered how nice she was to him, and her words of encouragement stayed with him every time he was in front of a crowd.

When he was in college, Jack had no idea where his future would lead him. He minored in journalism, but wasn't exactly the best writer; in fact, several professors adamantly warned him not take up writing as a full-time job. However, he now made quite a bit of advance money with his books, and they certainly turned out to be a lot of fun for him. Meeting parents who loved his books was so rewarding that he continued writing, and he had no intention of stopping now.

Morgan turned back toward Jack. "So, are you ready, Doc?"

Jack smiled and took one more long, deep breath. "You got it. I'm out of here."

"Okay, coming around. Have a good one."

Just as Jack was about to get out of the car, a little boy of about six, with curly black hair, ran smack into him. Following him was a beautiful, tall woman. She had beautiful big eyes, gorgeous curly dark hair, and a terrific smile. There was delicacy in her face, as well as strength. Something about her seemed so familiar.

"Oh my God, I'm so sorry," she said. "My son is a lot faster than me. His specialty is trying to run away from me, but that's not going to happen on my watch."

"Eventually, they all grow up," Jack said, just wanting to stand there and talk to this gorgeous woman with an overexcited kid. Her eyes kept him focused on her, but he knew the crowd was waiting.

Luckily, Jack blocked Andrew with his leg, and Morgan blocked him with his arm, so the boy didn't get to run any farther. He wasn't out of breath, but his mother was.

"Thanks so much," she said. "He's pretty darn fast."

"He's just got a lot of energy. Kids are like that," Jack said, flashing that perfect smile of his, and realizing he could have said something a little cleverer.

"This one's got a lot of energy. Big time! He keeps me on my toes." She stared at Jack as if she knew him, but she couldn't place him. There was something very familiar about his voice.

Jack's full attention was on the lovely woman standing before him, but he knew he had to move on. His agenda was supposed to be a book signing, not meeting a woman. He didn't even know if she was single, though that had never stopped him in the past. He looked at the little boy and asked, "What's your name?"

When the boy didn't answer, his mother did. "Guess he remembered not to talk to strangers. His name is Andrew."

He was about to kick Jack's leg, but Victoria clutched his hand before he could do it.

Jack was scrambling for words. He didn't want her to leave, but he had to go inside. "Why don't you both come in and be my guests?"

She didn't quite understand what he was doing there. "Your guests? For what?"

Jack held out his hand. "Dr. Jack Winston. I'm here for a book signing. And you are…"

"Victoria Hudson." She always used her maiden name when meeting people. "I'm on my way to my sister's office. Sorry. Have a good book signing."

"Are you sure you won't stay?"

"I'm sure. Nice meeting you, Jack."

Just as she walked away, she realized who he was. Her mother loved Jack Winston. That's why there was a familiarity—she had heard him interviewed a few times. Victoria walked on, still thinking about him.

Jack watched as Victoria and Andrew walked away. She was beautiful and he wanted to know everything about her, but he had a commitment and was going to honor it.

"I'll get some info on her," Morgan whispered. "I can tell you were interested."

"That would be perfect. How do you always seem to know what I need?"

Morgan laughed. "All in my job description, Doc. Go in and have a great signing. Give them what they want."

"You're right. I'm going in."

• • •

Jack was warmly greeted by the manager. He didn't recognize her at first, because she was a lot thinner and much more attractive. But when she whispered in his ear, he knew her voice. "You've come a long way from the bag of Cheetos and a near-empty room, don't you think?"

"Agnes Blackwell, is that you? You look great. I knew you found an audience for me that night. I never forgot, and probably never will."

Agnes was surprised that Jack remembered her. "You knew about the audience?"

Jack smiled. "Of course I knew. So, are we having Cheetos today?"

Agnes couldn't help but feel flattered. How could she not? She was standing with Jack Winston—not only a celebrity, but one absolutely gorgeous man. "No Cheetos today. This time, we're having cupcakes with sprinkles. Everyone loves a good cupcake. Besides, you're Jack Winston. You deserve to have five-dollar cupcakes at your book signing."

It was time and everyone was waiting, so Agnes nodded to her assistant, Pierce Lawrence, to begin. This was Pierce's first big event, and he was quite nervous as he walked out to the podium. He kept taking small breaths, in and out, focusing on why he was hired and what he needed to do.

"Hello everyone, and welcome to Maxwell Meyers." Those were the only words Pierce said before he froze. Luckily, there was so much commotion that no one except Agnes noticed. Her assistant had become pale, and she could tell he was seconds away from falling flat on his face.

Agnes quickly took the podium, trying to let Pierce off the hook. "Hello everyone," she began. "I'm so sorry we don't have enough seats, but we are going to do the best we can to accommodate all of you. We knew today would be one of the biggest signings we have ever had, but we had no idea we would be turning people away. Chicago's occupancy code is very strict. The good news is Dr. Winston has graciously informed me that he will come back next month. So let's show Jack some love. He's one of Chicago's own—Dr. Jack Winston!"

As Jack stepped beside Agnes, he politely smiled. "How do you know I'll agree to come back?" he whispered in her ear.

"Some things you just know." And when he smiled at her, she knew he would keep his promise.

Just before he was ready to go on, Jack looked out at the audience, thankful to have such loyal fans. Two hours later, after a long question-and-answer session, he strolled back to Agnes's office, where she handed him a glass of champagne. "To your career and my victory. Thanks so much for making this visit so special. You could feel the crowd loving you."

Pierce was lying on the couch; he had fallen fast asleep right after he screwed up his welcome speech. Jack was a little concerned, so he leaned over to check his vital signs. "Well, he's alive. His pulse is normal."

Agnes laughed. "He's fine. He faints when we have celebrities here. So far he hasn't been able to speak at a signing, but I keep him because he's a good guy. He's smart and he listens to all my crazy ideas. He's also very good in the sack, and very discreet. My husband never suspects a thing. Why would he? You know, it's those quiet ones…"

By this time, Jack realized she was sharing a little too much information, and he needed to leave. So he politely took a sip of champagne and called it a day. "Agnes, my dear, thank you so much for this wonderful afternoon. I know you went to a lot of trouble to make this a great signing, and it was. By the way, the cupcakes were terrific."

"So glad you came back. I always knew you would be a successful author."

"I'm glad you did; I wasn't quite sure. I promise to send you a list of dates when I can return."

Morgan was waiting for him, parked in a loading zone. Jack never liked when Morgan got out to open his door, so he motioned for him to stay right where he was. Still, Morgan got out of the car because he liked to do the right thing.

He was dedicated to Jack, having taken care of him ever since he was a little boy. Even when Jack's father died and money was tight, Morgan stayed on without a salary until Jack's mom landed on her feet. Even after all these years, he remained Jack's best friend and confidant.

"Okay, here's the skinny on your new beautiful brunette," Morgan said. "Her full name is Victoria Hudson Feingold. She's a divorced pediatrician and has three children, a mother, a sister, and a dog. They all live in Winnetka, in one house. If that's not enough information to keep you from going further, I don't know what is."

"How did you manage to find that out so fast?"

"If I told you my secrets, you wouldn't need me."

"Now that's bullshit. If I need anyone, it's you. You raised me."

"Let's give your mother some credit. She did what she had to. She married Alex Wainwright, rest his soul, so you could have a good life."

"Morgan, I've got to hand it to you. You always put everything in the right perspective."

"That's why you pay me the big bucks," Morgan said, laughing.

Jack thought for a few seconds. "Let's take a ride to Winnetka. It's a nice day."

"Maybe you should quit while you're ahead. You know your rules. No dating women with children. She has three kids, and it looks to me like she's got a house filled with a lot of people. You know how you like your quiet."

"Don't worry, Morgan. I'm just bringing her a book."

"It's never just a book."

"You're right, but this is different. There was something so familiar about Victoria. I want to know her better. It won't be just a date or a quick hop into bed. There's something about her. She certainly is beautiful, isn't she?"

Morgan was amused. "Yes she is. You keep saying that as if you haven't been with beautiful women. They've all been beautiful."

Jack had made up his mind. He was paying a visit to a woman he barely knew, a woman who got to him with her smile. In the past, he always assured himself that things happen for a reason and can't be questioned. After all, he was just dropping off a book. How serious could that be?

Chapter Three

The neighborhood where Victoria lived was quite beautiful. It had a mixture of large and small houses, all of them well kept. The lawns were manicured to perfection, and the trees were full and blossoming.

It was a quiet block where nothing out of the ordinary happened, at least until Jack's limo pulled into the driveway of Victoria's home. The neighbors knew it wasn't because someone had died—they would have already known that, as most of them read the obituaries daily.

Jack had always wanted to live on a block like this, where everyone knew each other. Instead, he grew up in a high-rise apartment, with more than ten thousand square feet of living space and a rooftop garden. It was featured in several highbrow magazines, which never meant anything to Jack.

As soon as Jack rang the bell, Grace greeted him with a surprisingly friendly handshake and a smile. "Oh my God, Jack Winston!"

"You know me?"

"Of course I know you! Actually, you look even better in person, if that's possible. You've been on the news all day. It's a big thing when a famous author comes to town. You know, you are a celebrity."

Jack laughed. "I live in Chicago. They keep telling me I'm a celebrity, but really I'm just a child psychiatrist who writes books."

"Well, not around here. So, now that we've got that out of the way, what on earth are you doing at my door-step? Come in."

Approaching them was an adorable schnauzer who seemed to own the place. He didn't just enter; he pranced. Angus was always there to greet every visitor. He wasn't exactly what anyone would call a watchdog or protector, but Angus could be very vocal if he didn't feel right about someone.

Jack felt a little uncomfortable as the little dog seemed to be checking him out. It was probably his imagination, but it seemed as if this dog was about to talk. "You have no idea what you're getting into," Jack thought he heard the dog say. "Once Grace starts talking, she just keeps on going." Jack blamed it on being a little tired from the after-signing questions at the bookstore.

"I came to bring your daughter a book. We ran into each other this afternoon. Actually, Andrew ran into me while Victoria was chasing after him."

"Sounds like Andrew," Grace said. "I didn't know my daughter knew you. She never mentioned you in any of our conversations. God knows I quote you all the time."

Angus gave him a look. "You'd better come up with something better than that, pal," the dog seemed to say. "Andrew? My goodness. Grace can see through you, so rise to the occasion and be honest."

Jack handed Grace a copy of his book. "Victoria was in such a hurry that she couldn't stay for the signing, so I thought, 'Why not bring her a book?' Is she home? I thought I'd say hello before I left."

"So sorry. She won't be home for a while. I'm Grace, and this little guy is Angus."

"Nice to meet you, Grace. You too, Angus." Jack leaned down and shook Angus's paw.

It almost looked as if Angus was smiling. Jack thought he had now legitimately reached the crazy limit. He had heard other writers talk about it.

By this time, Grace had a hunch Jack wasn't there just to bring one of his books, as he had the look of a man on a mission. She thought she would keep him there, and maybe Victoria would be home by the time there was nothing more to say. She knew Jack had lots of women, but no wife. Grace had read about it in the tabloids, so it had to be true. What a catch. If she were younger, he would certainly be staying for dinner, and possibly for breakfast.

"As long as you're here—and God knows, I'm happy you are—come with me." Grace took hold of Jack's hand and dragged him toward the library. "I have your books and, unlike my daughter, I have plenty of time to read. She never rests. It's no wonder she couldn't spare an hour to go to your book signing. I try to follow your advice, but my daughter has her own opinions on raising children. She needs to read your books. You are spot on."

For some reason, Jack felt quite comfortable talking with Grace, but he didn't want to say why he really came over. "I think I should get going. I've taken up so much of your time. Will you mention I stopped over?"

Grace took his arm again and walked him into the kitchen. "How about coffee? I just made some mandel bread. It's a Jewish cookie."

Jack laughed. "I know what that is. I love mandel bread, but I think I should be getting back. My driver is waiting outside."

"So tell him to join us. If he's a friend of yours, he's a friend of mine. If I have Jack Winston in my house, don't think I'm going to let him leave hungry."

Jack went to the door and motioned for Morgan to come in. It certainly appeared that his driver had made some new friends. Several senior women were conversing with him, and one even had her arm inside his.

Angus was right by Jack's side, whispering again. "Looks like your friend is having the time of his life."

Jack was a little surprised to see Morgan so jovial. This was a side of him that Jack had never seen. Morgan had finally let his guard down.

"Guess he doesn't have a hard time picking up women," Angus added.

Jack had unquestionably lost his mind, thinking that a dog could possibly be talking to him. He hadn't had a vacation in a while, and apparently he needed one. He had decided not to go to a medical convention in Vegas, but he was now rethinking that.

For the next hour or so, Grace entertained Morgan and Jack. By the time they had several cups of coffee and had eaten most of the mandel bread, the afternoon had passed quickly. Unfortunately, Victoria hadn't come home, but Ava arrived with Noah, Allyson, and, of course, Andrew.

Andrew ran into the kitchen and jumped on Jack, saying, "I know you."

Angus grabbed onto Jack's pants, hoping he would look down. "Take a deep breath and it will be over soon," the dog said. "They're not bad kids, just a little noisy. They're quiet when they sleep. Five hours and counting until bedtime."

Jack smiled, even though he didn't exactly love when kids jumped on him. Just because he wrote about children didn't mean he knew how to interact with them. His patients were usually teenagers.

Allyson, who was nine, walked into the kitchen, not paying the least bit of attention to anything other than the book she was reading. "Hi, Grammie," she said, grabbing a piece of mandel bread. She didn't look up or realize there were others in the room until she bumped into the wall and stubbed her toe. "Shit," she called out.

"Allyson," Grace said, "meet Dr. Jack Winston."

Allyson put down her book and politely shook Jack's hand. "Nice to meet you, Dr. Jack." She was a little embarrassed about what she had just said. Usually, the boys were the ones who swore no matter who was there.

Jack smiled, realizing he kind of liked being called "Dr. Jack." It sounded welcoming. He realized he was jumping way too far ahead. Just because he found their mother attractive didn't mean he would ever see Allyson, Noah, or Andrew again. He might not ever have a date with Victoria. And why was he even there? Three kids—he must be crazy. He had rules, but he was still there.

Noah ran in and hugged Grace. "Grammie, Grammie, Grammie, can I eat at Sam's house? We have homework to do. Lots of homework. And besides, they're having a cookout. You know, hot dogs, hamburgers, corn, marshmallows, chocolate s'mores…"

Grace gave him a look. "I know what a cookout is. Will you promise to do your homework?"

"I promise, Grammie."

Angus looked at Noah, who gave him a nod and a smile. Angus knew Noah had no intention of doing homework, and he wondered why Grace hadn't figured that out yet. But he was a dog, and what did he know about homework?

"Noah," Grace said. "Meet Dr. Winston."

Noah looked at Jack with a blank stare, then quickly inched his way out of the room. "Nice to meet you," Noah said. "Goodbye. Got to go."

"Sorry, Jack, he doesn't like doctors," Grace explained politely. "Been that way since he was a baby. He could sense when he was going for a baby checkup, and started crying in the parking lot at the doctor's office even before we got out of the car."

Jack laughed. "Believe me, he'll grow out of it."

"No worries," Angus whispered to Jack. "He doesn't like dogs either."

Ava had a few packages in her arms, which didn't allow any time for primping before she walked into the kitchen. When she saw two men there, she was sorry she hadn't put on any lipstick. "Gentlemen, I'm the evil sister, Ava Hudson. Nice to meet you."

Grace looked at her daughter, certain that Ava would go on and on if she didn't interrupt—and probably say something private, or at least unnecessary. "Ava, dear, meet Morgan and Dr. Jack Winston."

Morgan knew exactly who Ava was, because she was the one who gave him Victoria's address earlier that day. However, he told her Jack was going to mail a book, not go to the house. Ava recognized them immediately, and was very surprised to see them there. She knew she shouldn't have given out their address, although her mother always spoke of Jack Winston as if she knew him. Still, who was she to ruin the party?

"Hi guys!" she called out.

Morgan seemed a little preoccupied, but answered anyway. "Good to see you again, Miss Hudson."

Grace didn't seem to hear that, which was a good thing. Ava wasn't known for making great decisions, but her mother seemed quite entertained by the two of them—and Morgan seemed to be enjoying himself with her. Grace could be funny when she felt like it, but Ava knew she didn't bring out the best in her mother; they had more than their share of disagreements.

Jack seemed to enjoy watching Morgan interact with Grace. In all the years he had known him, Jack had never seen Morgan so full of life. Grace did have that special something that made anyone feel right at home. The way they were all talking, it felt more like a family conversation than one between a group of people who had just met.

Morgan had never been married, but he was a handsome guy over sixty with a thick head of white hair. He had bright green eyes, and very few wrinkles. At his age, he had all but given up on finding someone he could share his life with. Seeing him with Grace, Jack thought maybe this woman could change his friend's life forever.

As for Jack, he was a little disappointed that Victoria didn't come home. What he didn't know was she had seen his car outside and remembered it from the afternoon. She also saw several of her mother's friends milling around the front door, and the last thing she needed was an open house. After becoming very bored waiting for everyone to leave, Victoria drove away.

Chapter Four

While packing some last-minute things for a speaking engagement in Las Vegas, Victoria reminded herself of something else she had to do. Sometimes she put things off rather than face them head on, especially things concerning her ex-husband. She tried her best to keep her visits with Michael to a minimum, because she usually made him uneasy, but today she didn't care. She was a little tired of treating him with kid gloves.

Although he sometimes insisted her goal in life was to make him as miserable as he made her, Michael didn't really believe that. She never deserved what happened. Michael didn't like new things and had a hard time with change; that's why the divorce was so difficult for him to handle.

It wasn't that he loved Victoria, as much as he loved their life—she worked, and he gambled. What gambler wouldn't appreciate that? Victoria knew she had made things too easy for him. As a doctor, she was quite busy and so was he—at the racetrack. She wouldn't make that mistake again.

Michael Feingold was minding his own business, trying to wake himself up with a bowl of soup at his favorite restaurant, when he saw Victoria walking toward him. "Damn it, Victoria, not today," he mumbled to himself. "I'm not in the mood." Michael hadn't had a good night's sleep since his divorce a little more than a year ago. He was very lonely, and mad at himself for putting his family in jeopardy; he had never meant for the problem to get that serious. He leaned his head down, hoping his ex-wife wouldn't see him.

Victoria took a deep breath, promising herself not to be harsh. She knew Michael was trying to hide, and saw how ridiculous he looked trying to dodge her, but she just moved on in toward him. She knew she sometimes went too far, but she was still mad. Why wouldn't she be? Michael gambled more than he ever did anything else. She used to think he loved her and the kids, but when he gambled away all their savings and they almost lost their house, she didn't think he cared about anything other than the rush he got from gambling. Victoria always believed trust was the most important element in a marriage, and she would never be able to trust Michael again.

"Well, looks like nothing has changed with you," she began. "It appears that you haven't slept too much—or showered, for that matter. What the hell is with you? You need to get on that job train and find a way to make money."

"Would it be too much to ask for you to say hello before you start with everything I do wrong?" Michael replied. "I thought women liked rugged-looking men. Isn't that attractive to you?"

"No, I like men who take responsibility for their actions. It isn't about how they look."

Just as Michael was about ready to get up and walk away, Victoria grabbed hold of his arm. "Sorry, please stay. I want to talk to you for a few minutes."

"Fine. What can I do for you? And how did you know I'd be here?"

"It's Monday, and the soup of the day is mushroom barley. I think I know you pretty damn well. After all, we were married for twelve years."

"And I know you," he added, turning back to his soup.

"Michael, I have a favor to ask."

"Whatever it is, yes. Just ask and then leave. I just want to finish my soup with a little peace and quiet."

"You might not want to do it."

"You never ask me to do anything, so it must be important if you're here tracking me down. Just remember, we're not married anymore—you're not supposed to care if I shave, shower, eat, or whatever the fuck I do."

Michael just sat there staring at her, certain she had no idea how awful his existence had become. Since their divorce, he kept hoping that one day she would ask him to come home. He would leave his horrible walk-up apartment in a flash. Who would miss a place where the only sunlight came from a tiny window over a leaky faucet? The walls were gray, depressing, and in need of a paint job. The most exciting part of the day was when the coffee shop down the street had deliveries at four in the morning.

"Okay, tell me what you need."

"I'm speaking at a medical seminar in Vegas. Can you look in on the kids and my mom while I'm gone?"

"You hate speaking in front of crowds."

"I took it because the pay's great."

"Where's your sister going to be? She's good with the kids. And your mom, she loves it when you're gone. No rules to follow. You've always had a habit of telling us all what to do."

"Well, you must be very happy with your new life—no rules, no me. You can do whatever you want anytime, anywhere. To answer your question, Ava will be there, but you know my mother still waits on her. If she gets mad, Ava leaves and doesn't return for a few days. That's their dynamic. So can you help me out?"

"You must be desperate if you're asking for my help."

"No, it's just that you're their father and they love you. I know it's not comfortable when I'm around and you're there, so I'm giving you the opportunity to see them and make sure everything goes well."

Michael didn't answer her at first, because he couldn't help but wonder how he got to this place in his life. He had it all, and gave it up for a life of regret. He tried so many times to apologize for his horrific behavior, and for the financial mess he passed on to Victoria. He knew she had no use for him, but he still had feelings. He wasn't the bastard she thought he was.

"Of course I can help. Anything for you, Vic."

"Please don't call me Vic. It's too endearing."

"Heaven forbid I say anything lovable," he sadly added.

"You won't forget, will you?"

"You don't have much faith in me, do you? I love my kids, and you know I love you and always will. If you ask me to do something, I'll be there. I know I did some really awful things, but it doesn't mean I don't love my kids enough to make sure they're alright. I know you don't trust me, but I'm trying to regain your love and trust. You know I want you back, and I think you might want the same thing, but you're so stubborn."

That was her cue to leave. She promised never to let her guard down, no matter how hard it would be. Part of her still loved Michael, but there was nothing he could say or do that would allow her to act on that love. Losing everything once was enough.

"On that note, it's time for me to go. So I can count on you? I'll tell my mother."

"Vic, one more thing. I'm back at Gamblers Anonymous, and I think I might have gotten a job. It's not my dream job, but I'm going back to teaching and I'll get a check. Maybe we can start over. We're young enough to replace the bad memories with some good ones."

"You know we can't. This isn't about love; it's about my sanity and your recovery. We are never getting back together. Not now, not ever. You know it's too late for us. That ship has sailed."

Chapter Five

When Victoria got home, her kids were still up and her mother was on the phone. Grace stopped for a minute to give her daughter the book Jack had left, then continued with her conversation. In fact, Grace spent the rest of the night making phone calls, telling everyone she knew that Jack Winston had been to her house and that she had coffee with Jack and his driver. Victoria was pretty sure her mother would be up all night, as Grace was still on the phone when Victoria headed to bed.

Victoria decided to finish packing in the morning, realizing she needed some rest. But just as her head hit her pillow, her cell phone rang. She knew it was the hospital; she could always tell.

One of her patients, a six-year-old girl with a bad reaction to her chemo, needed her care. Victoria stayed with her the whole night. When she came home in the morning, she didn't have much time, and taking a shower was out of the question.

She turned up the music on her phone and listened to Aretha Franklin, the queen of soul, while she tried to pack. In Victoria's world, there was no song as good as Aretha's version of "Respect." After the night she had, she needed some chill time, and listening to music usually did the trick. Even though she knew she was late, she started to dance. It eased her mind and allowed her to unwind. As soon as the kids heard the music, they came running in and Angus tagged along. The kids danced and Angus ran around in circles.

As Victoria bent down, Angus whispered to her, "I think I'm getting too old for this."

"Me too," she added. Despite the fact that she was late, she still had time to hug Angus and give him a kiss. "What would I do without you?"

Angus gave her a look and said, "You'd probably have to talk to your family more."

"Then you'd better not die," she whispered, and kissed him again.

"Thought you'd be gone by now," Michael said as he entered, acting like everything was perfectly normal.

"Obviously. You're here pretty early for you."

"Didn't sleep much."

"Well, you're one up on me. Didn't sleep at all. Sick patient, but she's better now."

"Sorry about that. You can sleep on the plane."

"You know I hate flying. I won't be sleeping; I'll be praying."

For the first time in a long time, Michael laughed.

When Victoria looked over at Michael, she couldn't help but feel sorry for him. His father was also a gambler, and his mother left when he was an infant, so he grew up unhappy and very angry. He had gone for help when he was a teen, but nothing ever eased his pain.

Seconds after Michael arrived, things got a little crazy. The music was loud, and Victoria still hadn't finished packing. "Can everyone please leave my room?" she asked. "Otherwise, I'll never get out of here. I need to call the airport. I'm never going to make my flight, so I need to change it."

"I can change it," Ava volunteered, as she looked around the messy room.

Victoria knew she should have packed the night before, and now she was stuck with everyone in her room and nothing to wear. She wanted to scream, but didn't. She was very superstitious and hated flying, so she had her own rituals to follow—including never getting mad before a flight. The way she saw it, she didn't want to be remembered that way if she never came back.

When she was trying to be diplomatic, her sister's help was the last thing she wanted. "I don't think that's a good idea, Ava. Remember last time? When I got a room with no shower because my plane made three stopovers and they were all late?"

"One isolated incident. There was a shower down the hall."

"I know, I remember. There was also no soap in the bathroom. Shall I go on?"

Ava looked at her sister in the matter-of-fact way she had done so many times before. "Please do. I love to hear that story. You've told the damn story to everyone we know. Sometimes, even to strangers."

"Fine," Victoria said. "Just get me on the next flight out. I can be ready in half an hour. Thank you."

Victoria opened her suitcase, put it on the bed, and started throwing in her clothes. Her taxi was on the way. Since a shower had been ruled out, she sprayed herself with perfume, put on a dab of lip gloss, and was ready to go. She kissed her kids goodbye and ran out. Michael was standing there, wondering if she would kiss him good-bye too, but she didn't. "Michael, make sure everything is okay."

Grace was already outside with the cab. The taxi didn't look like it could make it to the airport, but Victoria just got in, figuring she would either die in the taxi or on the plane. With her attitude, it was a wonder she traveled at all.

Grace closed the door. "Don't worry, dear, I've got it covered. Your kids will be safe. Michael will help."

As Victoria looked back at her kids, she closed her eyes and prayed. "God watch over this house, because it looks like things are going to be up for grabs."

The cab driver looked back at her. "Are you okay?"

"I'm fine. I shouldn't ask this, but I will. How fast can you go? I don't want to be late. I already missed one flight."

"Not a problem, *Señorita*." He knew what she meant; this wasn't his first rodeo. He hit the pedal, and they were on their way.

The ride was a little bouncy, but it was the fastest trip to the airport that Victoria had ever had. She looked at her watch and took a deep breath. "You just saved my life."

"*Que dios este contigo.*"

Victoria turned back and smiled. "Meaning?"

"May God be with you," the driver translated.

"I hope so. Thanks."

The skycap looked at her ticket and told her to go ahead, since he would take care of everything. Victoria hoped he wasn't going to lose her luggage. Then again, she had no clue about what she had packed, so maybe it wouldn't be a total loss. She didn't even know if anything matched, but she would have to worry about that after she got to Las Vegas. The flight was boarding, so she ran.

When she got to the gate, everyone was in a hurry. Victoria took a minute just to catch her breath, waiting to be treated like cattle, but she wasn't. The flight attendants were so polite and sweet, she couldn't believe it. When she looked down at her ticket, she saw it was first class. Now she knew why they were so attentive and patient; she had paid for that luxury. Not that it wasn't great.

Victoria had time before the plane left the gate, so she called her sister. "How much?"

"My treat," Ava said. "Actually, it was Mom and me. We just added on. Remember, your ticket was part of the packet when you accepted the speaking engagement."

"And Mom knows?"

"Of course she knows. It was her idea."

There were very few people in first class, which Victoria was happy about. She was tired and somewhat crabby, but she figured napping for a couple hours would do the trick. Over the years, she had learned how to get by with very little sleep.

Getting everything ready for the trip had been overwhelming—getting her office ready for her departure, finding someone to take her calls, making sure the kids were all squared away with their schedules in place—but she knew all of this would be worth it. She would make substantially more money from speaking at the conference than she did for months of working in an office filled with crying babies and hospital rounds.

Pediatrics wasn't the highest-paying profession, but Victoria had grown to love it. Her first love was surgery, and she was one of the most promising surgeons in her class. However, being a good mother was her top priority, and surgeons had crazy schedules with too many emergencies. So she gave up her residency and went into pediatrics at a different hospital. She was good at her job, and when she left her office every night, she still had time to be there for her kids.

Victoria laid her head back, trying to relax. She never liked flying, but being in first class seemed to make her feel better. The seats were bigger and more comfortable, and the flight attendants were smiling. That, plus a Dramamine for her nausea, seemed to do the trick. Actually being alone was very exciting.

She hadn't gone anywhere since her divorce. She also hadn't had a chance to travel on vacation like her friends, because she had gotten married so young and started a family. She worked a lot of hours, and rarely had any alone time.

Victoria liked the idea of marriage and of sharing her life with someone special, but that wasn't exactly the way her marriage had been. Michael wasn't home much, and the kids took up all her spare time. Loving them was her top priority in life, and she was never sorry about that.

She knew she took the wrong road when she married Michael, and maybe someday the right man would be there for her, someone who actually listened and cared about the same things she did. She often wondered if there was someone like that out there—but if there wasn't, that would be okay. Marriage was the last thing on her mind.

She was so busy reminding herself of how alone she felt that she didn't realize a male flight attendant was staring at her, waiting for an answer. Apparently, he had asked a question, but she didn't hear him.

"Can I get you anything?" he repeated. "A cocktail, a soft drink, coffee, or tea?"

"A water would be nice." Victoria thought she could get used to this treatment. She almost forgot she was on a plane.

She smiled at him as he handed her a beautiful crystal glass, with a slice of lemon added to the water. Victoria knew this was going be a great flight. She almost wanted to call her mother and sister to thank them, but decided to wait until she got there in one piece. Sometimes, she wished her superstitious side would go away. Instead, she closed her eyes and prayed as the plane took off.

After the seatbelt sign went off, and just as Victoria was ready to again close her eyes and try to forget she was in the air, Jack Winston was standing in the aisle with a drink in his hand. "Wine to relax?"

"Sounds good, but I don't drink. How did you know I needed to relax?"

"I was at your house yesterday, and met your mom, your sister, and your three children. Need I say more? Can I sit?"

Victoria decided not to tell him she knew he was there, or that she was outside but didn't want to come in. He probably wouldn't understand. She figured that her sister was the one who willingly gave out her address to strangers. That was Ava. Thinking things through wasn't one of her strong suits.

"Sure," Victoria said. "Not a problem. I might fall asleep. If I do, it's not your fault. Just had a bad night."

"Bad date? I've had many of those."

She smiled. "Wish it was that, but it was a very sick little girl. I'm a pediatrician. It was rough going, but it's all good now. She went through some pretty horrible treatments and has gotten really sick after each one, but this was pretty tough on her system. She's doing okay today, but we almost lost her."

"I know all about what you do for your patients. Your mother told me how dedicated you are."

"I suppose you know way too much about me. That's one of my mother's favorite topics, her daughter the doctor. My parents worked hard to make sure I got a great education, and I really do appreciate everything they did for me. She thinks I'm special, but I'm not. I just want to help my patients, and I tend to comfort them if they're really sick. Honestly, most of them are healthy, happy kids."

Jack couldn't take his eyes off her as she talked. She was even more beautiful when she got serious. Where had she been hiding all these years?

Victoria also seemed impressed with Jack. He was really good looking, not like most of the guys she knew. He was the real deal, the total package, and incredibly tempting. She didn't know that much about him until her mother gave her his book. She knew she had to wait until her seminar was over before reading Jack's book, but she couldn't help but Google him. That's how she learned all about his personal life. From what she saw, most of it was probably true.

Just as Jack couldn't take his eyes off her, she couldn't take hers off him. No wonder he had so many dates. Who wouldn't want him? His profile was sharp and confident, his eyes were magnetic, his smile was friendly, and he smelled great. Victoria was never really interested in any man since her divorce, but Jack was so charming she felt compelled to talk to him, and couldn't help but wonder what it might feel like to kiss him. She was sorry she hadn't taken the time to shower.

Jack was totally enamored with her. He had been with many women, but for some reason, he wanted to know everything about this one. She was beautiful and smart, and he was very attracted to her.

Usually, the initial hello was all he needed to know if there was a connection, but he knew he would have to work to get Victoria's attention. He liked that about her. There was a lot more to her than any of the others. He had a feeling in the pit of his stomach every time he looked at her, which for him was quite unusual. They continued talking, until they were interrupted by one of the flight attendants.

"Dr. Winston, it's such an honor to have you with us," the flight attendant said. "I wanted to thank you for your books. I refer to them the way some people refer to the bible. I couldn't have gotten through some tough times without your words of wisdom."

"It's so nice to hear you like my books," Jack replied. "I really appreciate that."

"You probably get sick of hearing that," she added.

"I never get sick of hearing that. Thanks so much."

"Would you autograph this for me?" She handed Jack a napkin, which he signed.

"I can do one better. Write down your address, and I will send you an autographed book."

"I'm a single parent and have been learning not to panic over situations that eventually work out. Reading your book is like having a husband without all the bullshit."

Jack couldn't help but laugh. "No one has ever put it quite that way before."

Victoria couldn't help but find the flight attendant's words amusing; she thought of Michael and realized they were quite true. Michael was harder to raise than her children.

Suddenly, there was air turbulence. In a flash, the attendant left them and went back to her seat, and the seatbelt sign began flashing. Making matters worse for Victoria, the pilot came on the loudspeaker. She liked it better when the pilot was flying rather than talking. Even though she knew there were two pilots in the cockpit, she hated to hear anything other than the temperature and time.

She was so busy talking to Jack that she had stopped thinking about the flight, but at that moment she didn't care how good looking he was. She started to pray. Damn, she hated flying. Her Dramamine wasn't working, probably because she only took half. Any more would have put her in a stupor, and she didn't want that to happen. Suddenly, she wanted to get up and go to the bathroom, but she couldn't. She was terrified—so much so that she vomited all over herself. She was embarrassed, but she couldn't help herself. She kept hoping this was all a dream, and that she could wake herself up.

Jack was trying to be macho, but he was scared to death. He also hated flying, which was one of the reasons why he had a few drinks. He needed to relax. Then there was a serious jolt, causing the plane to shake. It was moderate at first, then severe.

For fifteen seconds, it seemed as if the world was ending. The plane rocked, and Jack and Victoria felt as if they were dying. The storm caused the plane to plunge thirty feet. A few seconds later, everything was clear and they were on their way.

Once everything quieted down, Victoria left to go to the bathroom. She hated the confined area airlines called a bathroom; it was more like a closet. She had to get the smell off her clothes, but it just wasn't happening.

There was a knock on the door, and the flight attendant handed her a shirt. "I have an extra."

Victoria wanted to thank her, but first had to get rid of the horrible odor. The soap didn't smell great, but it was good enough. She threw her shirt in the garbage and put on the clean one. As Victoria leaned out the bathroom door, the attendant actually handed her toothpaste, saying, "I got you covered, honey."

After that, everything seemed easier for Jack and Victoria. They talked mostly about kids and their work. When they were finished talking, Jack took hold of Victoria's hand, and she didn't mind. Victoria felt safe, and Jack felt comfortable. Silently, each of them began to feel an unexpected bond. Neither of them ever thought sparks could fly with just a simple touch, but they did.

"So now that you're relaxed and we are staying at the same place, let's have dinner and celebrate being on the ground," Jack suggested once they landed.

Victoria wanted to say yes, but she wasn't on the ground yet. At that moment, dinner was something she wasn't thinking about—for that matter, she didn't know if she'd ever feel like eating again. "Besides," she asked, "how did you know where I am staying?"

"Wherever the conference is being held is where most of the doctors stay. It's just easier."

"I've got to be up early tomorrow. I need to write some opening and closing remarks. That's not my specialty."

Jack was disappointed when she said no, but he hoped she would change her mind. They had another day to unwind. "How about this? Just dinner, nothing fancy. You have to eat. I can help with your notes."

That sounded very appealing to Victoria, because she hated to write speeches. "Okay, just dinner, but I'm not too hungry right now. Are you?"

Jack didn't have to think twice before shaking his head.

Their passion was mounting, but neither of them would admit to feeling the urge to kiss. Victoria knew she couldn't complicate her life by falling for anyone. She was just beginning to learn how to live without Michael. Jack, on the other hand, had one essential rule when it came to women. Children were terrific and he loved them, but a ready-made family was not in the cards. So he and Victoria said their goodbyes, knowing that they would be having dinner that night, and each certain it was just dinner.

Jack had a car waiting for him, and was amused watching Victoria try to hail a cab. He waved her over, and she reluctantly agreed. She was tired and didn't want to wait around.

Once they were inside the car, everything changed. All of their crazy feelings came into play. As Jack moved closer, Victoria removed her jacket, lucky she had changed her shirt. Jack motioned for the driver to close the partition for privacy, something Morgan would have done automatically.

He began to trace his finger across Victoria's lips. The gentleness of his touch roused her passion. She took hold of his tie and quickly pulled it off. She was more aggressive than she had ever been. She felt her defenses weaken, and she was his. The afternoon ended nicely, totally unlike what each had imagined when they woke up that morning.

• • •

Checking in was a lot more difficult than Victoria imagined. There were so many people in line that it seemed as if it would be bedtime by the time she got settled. Happily, the reservations were honored, unlike some of the accommodations her sister had arranged. She was sometimes surprised some of the rooms Ava booked even had soap.

Jack waved goodbye as he was escorted by three bell-men. It definitely seemed like everyone knew him. In a few minutes, Victoria's room was ready.

Dinner was at eight, and Victoria didn't have a thing to wear. Nothing matched. When she left her house, she knew she hadn't packed anything special and might have to go shopping. After her fantastic afternoon—not including the turbulence, of course—she wanted to wear something beautiful and sexy. So instead of imagining that she could make anything she had work, she decided to hop in the shower, then run downstairs to the shops in the arcade and get something new.

Her phone kept ringing, but she didn't answer. Whoever it was could wait. It was most likely her mother or sister; a day didn't go by when they didn't call her at least ten times. The real kicker was sometimes they both called her at work at the same time, even though they were in the same house.

The water against her body felt good. She needed this time alone to capture the essence of what had happened in the limo. She had seen things like that in the movies, but never expected to have sex with a man she barely knew. More importantly, she loved that she had that experience. She hadn't felt that sexy ever before. She almost felt like it was an out-of-body experience.

"What a day," she thought.

After her shower, Victoria called down to the spa and made an appointment for her hair and nails, something she rarely did. Jack had brought back feelings she thought she had lost. She had been feeling somewhat like a mechanical human, programed to get up in the morning and do exactly what she had done the day before. Something like the movie *Groundhog Day*.

Jack was deliciously dangerous for her. He could have any woman he wanted, and she was just ordinary, so it would be presumptuous to think they could have anything more than a getaway fling. She would end it tonight, before either of them got hurt—something she feared immensely. She threw on her clothes, grabbed her bag, tossed her phone inside, and went off to the spa.

Chapter Six

Her phone rang a few more times, but Victoria still didn't answer. Just as she reached the elevator after having her hair and nails done, she heard a familiar voice say, "You're looking more beautiful than ever."

When she turned around, there was Michael. "What are you doing here?" she asked.

"Good question. Where are you off to?"

"Is this really something you think I need to answer? You go first."

"Well, have you talked to your mother?"

"What does my mother have to do with this?"

"I told her it was a bad idea. She planned a family trip at the same time as your speaking engagement. Did you even take time to remember that today is your thirty-fifth birthday?"

Victoria couldn't believe she forgot, but she had. When she was a kid, she loved her birthday. In fact, she used to stay up all night waiting to open her gifts. "I really forgot. I've been a little busy these days."

"Well, might as well brace yourself, because your mother, your sister, and our kids will be here tomorrow. I wasn't supposed to tell you, but I had to. I know how you hate surprises. So are you good with this?"

"No I'm not. And for your information, my life is one big surprise after another. Why are you really here?"

"Your mom thought that maybe, if we were together in a different situation, possibly we could…"

"There is no 'we.' This wasn't my mother's idea, was it?"

"Your mom did plan this day, minus me. She wanted to make your day special. Have you forgotten everything you once cared about?"

"Probably. Could you blame me?"

"No, I guess not. If I did that to you, I'm really sorry. I never wanted to ruin your life; I just wanted to be in it. Will you ever be able to forgive me?"

"I don't know. I really don't. Let's put it this way. It will take a long time and a lot of hard work to forget everything, but I'm going to do it."

Without thinking about the consequences, Michael gathered her into his arms and kissed Victoria in a way he had never done before. He took her breath away, and she was mad at herself for liking it. He confused her thoughts—just when she was enjoying thinking about Jack, her ex-husband showed up. He had already taken away too many of her years, and it was really nice thinking about another man.

"Michael, please go home. I should never have even mentioned my trip, but I just wanted you to keep an eye on my mother and the kids. Obviously, you're not doing that."

When the elevator door opened, Victoria walked in and pressed the button really fast, just to make sure Michael didn't follow her.

From the very moment Victoria met Michael, he always had an uncanny way of showing up and interfering with her life. Finally, the day had come when she felt free enough—and instead, Michael was right smack in her face and her whole family was on its way. What were the odds of that?

It had been quite a long time since Victoria had been with a man other than Michael, and she had often wondered if she would ever be able to be with someone else—but that afternoon, all the questions and fears were over.

She never remembered having sex like that with Michael. Most of the good times were erased by her anger. Her life was changing and—as much as she wanted to begin again—she was very afraid of what path she would go down. What if the same thing happened again? Would she be too busy to notice if things went bad? She had done it before, and now she was paying a big price for that.

Right then, Victoria stopped herself. She had to remind herself over and over that she hadn't done anything wrong. She had to put her bad memories aside and try to have fun. That was a tall order for her. First on her agenda was getting something to wear.

• • •

As she entered the boutique, Victoria felt so out of date. Because she had so many bills and so much debt from Michael's gambling, she hadn't looked at fashion as something important—paying for food and the house was first on the list. The boutique was upscale couture, totally unlike anything Victoria had in her limited wardrobe. She so was busy viewing everything, from the glamorous belts and scarves to the jewelry and hair ornaments, that she didn't see the sales associate behind her, and jumped when she spoke.

"So sorry, didn't mean to scare you," the associate said. She gave Victoria the once-over. "My dear, you are a pretty woman who needs to be pampered and dressed. My name is Monique. And you are?"

"Victoria Hudson, and I need help. I think you probably figured that out the moment you looked at me."

"What brings you here, hon? Just some fun?"

"I'm a doctor, and I'm speaking at the medical convention here. Tonight, though, I need something really fabulous. I want to look sexy."

"Terrific. What are you looking for?"

"I don't know, but I know I need something new."

"You're right about that. Why don't you tell me what you want to look like, or who you want to look like?"

"I want to look sexy, but not too sexy."

Monique laughed. "Not something I haven't heard before. This is Vegas. You're at the right place."

Victoria's phone kept ringing, but she let it go to voicemail. She didn't even check to see who was calling; it had to be her mother. By the time Victoria quit thinking about it, Monique had brought her six different changes, so Victoria could find her comfort zone.

Again the phone rang. "Hello, Mom."

"I've been called a lot of things in my life, but that was not one of them. It's Jack."

"So sorry. I've just been running around. No time for the nap I promised myself."

"Can we meet for a drink before dinner?"

"Sure. When and where?"

"About fifteen minutes? There's a small pub in the middle of the casino. Are you okay with that?"

"I'll be there. See you then."

Victoria took a deep breath. Luckily, there was a chair in the dressing room that she could plop into. She looked at herself in the mirror, almost forgetting why she was there. She was just about ready to leave when Monique ran after her.

"Where are you going? You haven't tried on anything yet."

"I have to meet someone in the lounge in fifteen minutes. No time for clothes shopping."

"A good someone? Or just someone?"

"Don't know yet. I think a good someone."

"Well, then sit yourself down and give me ten min-utes." Like a bat out of hell, Monique pulled a few different things from the back. She grabbed a brush, some spray, and her makeup bag. "Put this on," Monique said. "When you're done, I'll give you the one-two-three glamor look."

Victoria was far out of her comfort zone, so she just did as Monique said. She wanted to look good for Jack, which in itself was ironic. Impressing guys was never her thing. Even during college, she didn't care. She had always been about studying and more studying.

She put on the black leather pants and white lace shirt. She buttoned the shirt, zipped the pants, took a quick look, and she was ready. Monique insisted she sit down and take deep breaths until her new look was fin-ished. In another few minutes, Victoria's hair was pinned up by a beautiful comb, and her lips were glossed a pale pink. Her eyes were lightly shadowed and her lashes were lengthened by black mascara. Her cheeks were splattered with a natural baked blush. All in all, she looked pretty good for a doctor and mother of three in need of a good night's rest.

Just as she was ready to leave, Monique looked down at Victoria's feet. "Oh dear, your shoes. What size are you?"

"Seven."

Monique took off her Valentino pumps, put some tissue inside, and handed her shoes to Victoria. "Now you're ready. You look damn sexy. Go for it."

Victoria kissed Monique's cheek. "Are you this nice to everyone? I feel like a fairy godmother just dressed me for the ball."

"Damn straight, my dear. I'm a pay-it-forward kind of girl. But remember something—I'm no fool. Bring back my shoes, or my mean streak comes out. I can be your fairy godmother, but hell hath no fury when it comes to Valentino pumps."

"Do you know how to bill me?"

"I do. I checked you out while I was in the back. We have great security here. Besides, my daughter works at the front desk. You checked in a little while ago, am I right? Remember, this is Vegas, not too much is over-looked. The powers that be see to that."

Victoria smiled back at her and was on her way. She looked at her watch, realizing she might be late, and that maybe Jack wouldn't wait. She wished she didn't worry so much.

As she entered the casino, she looked around at everyone having fun and couldn't help but think about how horrible her life had become because Michael was a gambler. As she moved through the crowd of people, she wondered how many of them had almost lost their homes because someone wasn't watching. Her love had been blind, and she didn't think she had to keep an eye on Michael. She would never let that happen again. Today was a new day, with a new man, and it was going to be good.

• • •

There he was, sitting at the bar—Jack Winston, looking so gorgeous that Victoria had to step back and take a deep breath. She hadn't planned this day, but it sure was good for her. She had planned to live the rest of her life alone, and had decided she was through with men, so she was surprised by her feelings for someone she barely knew. Right at that moment, she felt good, surprised that she actually felt life changing. The black cloud seemed to be lifting; she had weathered the storm.

She was walking toward Jack when she noticed the guy sitting right next to him. Michael. They seemed to be having one hell of a conversation, and Victoria felt a chill move through her. She was ready to faint, but didn't. Instead, she decided to get out of there as quickly as possible. She could just leave and live the rest of her life celibate. No harm done. She would return her clothes, including her comfortable Valentino pumps. Then she would go upstairs to her room, order some dinner, revamp her speech, and go to bed. She decided she suddenly wanted to be a nun. If not for the fact that she was Jewish and had three kids, that plan could have been a good one.

Then again, Victoria loved being in love, and getting a divorce was the last thing she had ever wanted. She used to be certain Michael was the only man she would ever love. Now she wondered if Michael would always be around to ruin things. She really wished he hadn't come to Vegas.

As she headed back the way she came, Michael ran after her. The more he chased, the faster she ran. When he finally caught up with her, he could barely speak. "You look incredible," he said.

"Thanks, but I've got to go. Nice of you to notice, but you shouldn't be here in the first place."

"Don't go. There's someone I want you to meet. We went to school together."

"Really? Thank you, but no thank you. I have a speech to practice."

As always, Michael was determined. "Come with me for a second. Please."

Victoria began to feel her heart race. She realized that if she didn't leave right at that moment, she would once again allow herself to be manipulated by Michael. "Michael, stop. You need to go. We're divorced. You know you shouldn't have come. Why you did is still a mystery to me."

"Come on. It's Jack Winston. Your mother loves him. She has all his books. You met him at my fraternity house years ago, but you were both a little drunk."

"Really? I don't remember that. Did you just make that up?"

"No, of course not. Jack's a great guy. He became a very successful doctor and I didn't, as you know. He writes these books about kids."

"How lovely for him. Now if you'll excuse me, I have some things to do. What hotel are you staying at? Or should I assume you planned on staying with me?"

"Well, we never had problems with that part of our marriage."

"You're not staying with me. Just go back home. Please. Whatever you thought was going to happen here isn't going to happen."

Their conversation ended when Victoria got a text message from Jack. "Where are you? I'll come to you."

She texted back. "Meet me in the deli on the first floor, near the gift shops."

Victoria didn't know what to do, but she couldn't be with Michael. "You really shouldn't be here," she told him. "A casino is not on the Gamblers Anonymous list of places to visit. Why would you be here when you have a gambling problem?"

"There's only one reason I came here, and it wasn't to gamble. I want you back. I need you. We used to be good together."

"Well, we're not anymore. You know that." She brushed her hand across his cheek. "You will always be a part of my life, but not in the way you want. Let's just leave it at that. Please go."

Michael was numb, and stood motionless as he watched Victoria walk away. He knew it was over. He just had to be sure.

Suddenly, he felt a nudge. "How did it go, lover boy?" said a voice Michael recognized. "Was she happy to see you? I would be."

Michael didn't quite understand. "Why are you here? I thought you said you weren't coming."

"I knew I was coming. I knew you would need me."

His ex-sister-in-law, Ava, happened to look stunning. She usually wore layers of clothes, and her hair was always pulled up in a ponytail. Michael assumed he had one too many drinks, so he ignored how sexy he thought she looked in her red lace dress. The fact that her breasts were almost completely exposed surprised him, but they did look appealing. Her dark, curly hair was flowing down to her shoulders. Her lips were full and very sensual.

It all reminded Michael of their relationship many years ago. She was one hot chick in bed, but out of bed she was Victoria's sister. She had been off limits for a long time.

Ava had been the one who introduced him to Victoria, though only after she was through with him. Once Michael met Victoria, he fell in love with her, and that was that. He was angry with himself for even thinking about Ava, although he was glad to see someone didn't hate him.

"You wanted to know how it went?" he said. "Not well. Your sister doesn't want me, and I don't blame her, but I want what we had."

"Michael, you had a lot of bad days together." Ava took his hand. "Did you ever think you might not have been right for each other?"

"No, never."

"Maybe you should. It's time for some fun. Let me tell you something. I love my sister, but you were never right for her. I know what you need. I always did. When we met, I was just too damn young to know it."

"I'm not staying, Ava. She doesn't want me to. I shouldn't be here, and I don't know why I even came. Victoria's right. I need to move on. I think I'll go back to Chicago tonight. Thanks for the ticket. It just didn't work."

"The hell you will. We're in Vegas, You're not going home yet. My mother and the kids will be here in the morning. And it did work. I knew it wasn't going to go well. You just needed to see it for yourself."

Michael was a little confused by this whole chain of events. "Why are you here?"

"Truth?"

"Yes. Truth."

"Later. Now let's have some fun."

"Ava, did you plan this?"

"Some of it."

"I don't even have a room."

Ava handed him a key. "You sure as hell do. Mine. I won't take no for an answer. They gave me a suite this time, making up for the mistakes they made in the past, so let's live it up. We're going to get free food and drinks and a very glitzy room, with a perfect view of the strip."

"Not so sure this is a great idea."

"It's a terrific idea." Ava was certain of that. Now all she had to do was prove it to Michael— which could take a little time, because he was not in the best of spirits. She knew him very well, certainly a lot better than he thought. She had promised herself long ago that if Michael ever became free, really free and clear, she would make her move. She had lived far too many years thinking she let a good one go. She could cut through the bullshit a lot faster than her sister.

Chapter Seven

When Victoria got to "shoppers row," as she called it, she couldn't believe there were so many expensive shops. She had never liked shopping, which was another reason why she wouldn't be winning any best-dressed contests.

Jack had made her feel special, but she imagined he had a knack for that. She had seen him in several "who's who" columns with beautiful and famous women, and she was definitely not the trendy type. She kept to herself as much as she could, and hoped that Jack wouldn't miss the dazzling beauties he was used to.

When Victoria didn't see Jack, she wondered if he had a change of heart. After all, she had so much baggage weighing her down that most men would probably turn away and not look back. She loved having three children, but would a man without any be able to handle such a challenge? She paced back and forth, hoping he would turn up, while also nervously hoping that Michael wouldn't. She was sure that what she'd had that afternoon was just sex, plain old everyday sex. Something that didn't need any explanation. It might never happen again. Then again, it could happen as early as that night.

Just then, Jack texted her. "I'm upstairs. Room 1024."

She took a deep breath and headed on up. She exhaled several times, trying to catch her breath. Victoria had a history of hyperventilating when she was nervous. When she was with patients, she was calm and clear, but in her personal life she was nervous and unsure. As a doctor, her patients were always her first priority, and she never let her personal problems overshadow their care. In medical school, she was always at the top of her class, and the best at whatever rotation she was working. She was a terrific doctor and proud of that. Romance was another story.

When the elevator stopped at the tenth floor, Victoria got out. But on her way to the room, she changed her mind and headed back toward the elevator. Jack had been watching her from down the hall, and ran over. "Victoria where are you going? Wait up."

"Jack, I think I made a mistake. I shouldn't be here. We're two adults and we just had sex a few hours ago. It was good, I might add, but we should leave it at that."

"Are you always this hard on yourself?"

"Yes. I actually was born that way. It's my heritage. Can't help myself."

"I have that same heritage. Not every Jew is tough on themselves."

"In my family, we are. Well, all of us except Ava. So that's why you need to move on. We shared a bad flight and some good sex, but anything other than that would be a mistake."

Jack stopped her. "Maybe I could get a word in, if possible."

"Sure. Go ahead. Another reason not to be with me. I talk too much."

Victoria stood there, looking so beautiful that all Jack wanted was to hold her in his arms and tell her it was all okay. He knew the minute he laid eyes on her that she was a force to be reckoned with, and he just wanted to be with her. He didn't need one hundred reasons otherwise. It certainly shocked him that he didn't want to run, even after he met her family.

When they walked back to his room, he suddenly realized that not only was he barefoot and shirtless, but he'd forgotten his entry card and the door had locked.

Victoria took out her cell and handed it to him. "I'll just call down."

While they waited, Victoria eased down and sat on the carpet. Jack joined her and took her hand.

"Look, this is new for me," he said. "I actually don't know how to act. All I know is there is something about you that makes me happy. Sitting here right now, it seems like I could get used to waking up every morning next to you. And believe me, that's new for me."

"It's new for me too, and it's not just me. It's my kids, my mother, my sister, and Angus. It's all of us. We fight, and we fight some more. No matter what, we love each other."

Just then, the bellman arrived. He reached down and handed Jack another entry card. Jack was surprised the hotel just gave him the card with no ID, until the bellman handed him a pen and paper and asked, "Can I have your autograph?"

Jack signed the paper in amazement. He was always shocked that everyone seemed to know him.

"My wife and I have read every book you wrote," the bellman said. "Thank you. We are a happy couple because of your help. We used to fight about how we would raise our boys. Now we've got a path to follow."

As soon as the bellman left, Jack pulled Victoria toward him and kicked the door shut. He lifted her up against the wall and their passion was obvious. By no means was this just a fling. Victoria knew that she couldn't resist; something inside her changed the moment she met Jack.

They seemed to know each other a lot better than either of them expected. Jack paused for a second to look at her. He whispered her name and she whispered his. As the excitement grew, there was a momentary tingling in the pit of her stomach that she had never had before, even with Michael. As for Jack, he had fallen in love; this was the woman he wanted to marry.

Victoria's phone rang, but she didn't answer. She let it go straight to voicemail.

When they were finished, Victoria glanced over toward the sofa, saw the clothes she had bought for the evening, and smiled. "So much for dressing for dinner."

She was overwhelmed. Nothing like that had ever happened to her.

"We can go out for dinner or order room service. Or better yet, we're in Vegas—we can get married." Jack shocked himself when he it. "Yes, let's get married. It's no problem getting someone to officiate. There's a chapel on every corner."

"You know Michael, right? He was in the bar with you."

"I do. He mentioned you. Mostly that he loved you and wanted you back."

"Did you say anything about us?"

"No, not a word. That's a conversation for you to have with Michael, not me."

Victoria knew it was something they should talk about. "Okay. Just so you know, there is absolutely no chance of me getting back together with Michael. Did he tell you what happened?"

"He did. I'm so sorry."

Victoria grabbed her clothes from various locations, wishing she was invisible. Jack walked over toward her, trying to stop her from cleaning up. "The room comes with maid service," he said.

"I clean when I'm upset. And yes, I will marry you. I've never done anything like this before."

"Me neither. I'm crazy about you, and this whole thing is so new to me. I just want to be with you. I can't remember ever feeling this way, and this whole thing scares me to death. Do you remember meeting me years ago?"

"No, but when I saw you outside Maxwell Meyers, there was something about you that seemed so familiar. It wasn't only because you're handsome and charming, not that that's a bad thing. I was sorry I didn't go in when you asked me."

Jack smiled. He felt a little disappointed that she didn't remember him, so he felt compelled to fill her in. "We were hanging out on the lawn at a frat house party and you were sitting on the grass all by yourself. And, if I might add, you looked stunning. I couldn't keep my eyes off you, but you didn't say anything. You just sat there."

"I didn't say anything? Really?"

"Nope, not a word. But you smiled at me when I kissed your cheek, and I never quite forgot that."

Victoria was beyond flattered. "We barely know each other, but I feel as though you've always been in my life. How weird is that?"

"So, Doctor Victoria Hudson Feingold, rumor has it that you will marry me."

For a few seconds, they stood there, staring at each other. Finally, Jack broke the silence. "This is reckless, isn't it?"

"Yes it is, but it's kind of spontaneous. My sister did things like this. Used to drive my parents crazy, but I kind of envied it. My father used to call Ava his 'Miss Spur of the Moment,' and me 'Miss Sensibility.' I used to think it was a compliment, but it might have become my greatest liability. Talking about it now, it just seems as if I'm boring. Maybe it's time to just go for it. After all, life is short."

Jack bent down on one knee. "Dr. Victoria Hudson, will you marry me tonight? Believe me, this is going to be a chance for both of us to have it all, love and happiness. You did say yes, Doctor, didn't you?"

Victoria wrapped her arms around him. "Yes, I did say yes, Doctor."

Jack took her hand. "Let's go. You have a speech to give tomorrow."

"And I'm looking forward to you writing it. That's one good to reason to marry you. You're a writer, or at least that's what everyone tells me. Of course, that's not the only reason I'm marrying you. There are other reasons, I just don't know them yet. I hope you're not a murderer. Oh boy, I've become Grace. That sounded just like my mother."

Jack stopped dead in his tracks. "Well, I'm not a murderer. That's one thing out of the way. Also, my dear, you are not boring. You're just right. What's wrong with smart and beautiful?"

"Nothing. We're going to do this, aren't we?"

"We are, and I'm happy. Even though it might sound crazy, sometimes you've got to be a little crazy."

"Said the psychiatrist to his future bride."

Chapter Eight

Morgan called Grace right after Victoria left for her trip. She was flattered that he wanted to see her, and at that point she had no idea that Jack was going to be in Vegas at the same time as her daughter.

She couldn't accept his invitation for a night out because she thought leaving the kids might not be a good idea, but inviting him for dinner was the least she could do. She felt an attraction to him. She wasn't about to act on it, but as long as he was the one who initiated their meeting, she was happy. Dinner was a good way to start. She knew the way to a man's heart was through his stomach, regardless of his age.

Morgan had worked for Jack's family for most of his adult life. Now that he was older, he realized he really didn't like being alone. Sixty was the new forty. So he graciously said yes to dinner, remembering Grace's wonderful Jewish cookies.

If she could make such wonderful cookies, she would certainly be a great cook. He loved a good homemade meal, especially when he didn't have to make it. Jack was usually out for dinner or working late hours, and Morgan didn't like to eat late. Usually, he just went to a diner or stayed home to eat popcorn and watch old movies.

He was a little disappointed when he got there and found out that dinner was hot dogs, potato chips, and pickles. It smelled like being at the ballpark, which he did like, but it was not what he was expecting. Morgan was very set in his ways—especially his eating habits—but didn't want to be unappreciative, so he joined Grace and the three kids at the dinner table.

It was a little noisy, and sort of gross. But just the same, he felt happy when he was with Grace. It wasn't a fluke that he was falling for a woman he barely knew; he really liked her. When the kids were done eating and went into the other room to watch television, Morgan and Grace conversed while cleaning up. She made him laugh, and he loved it.

"So, Morgan, why are you here? Not that I wasn't flattered when you called, but I didn't expect to hear from you. What gives?"

"Do you want the truth?"

"Of course I do. Unless it's bad. Then I prefer lies."

"I haven't been with a woman in a very long time. But from the moment I laid eyes on you, I wanted to take you in my arms and hold you there for the rest of my life."

Grace, who usually had a lot to say, couldn't speak. She just stood by the sink, so shocked by his candor that she couldn't move. Morgan stood up, realizing he said too much too fast, but Grace ran after him. "Don't go. You can't leave after saying the most beautiful words any man has ever said to me, and that includes my late husband." She looked up, as if to address him. "Sorry, Maurice, my dearly departed. It's true."

Morgan was a little nervous, not sure what he should do next. He wasn't exactly a man with experience, but Grace understood. She moved closer to him. "Well, here we are, just you and me," she said. "So show me what you would have done yesterday if you and I were left alone."

He was very tall, and Grace was not even five feet with her shoes on. Morgan was a big man—not fat, just put together very well for a man his age. Looking at him excited her, and she felt something she had thought impossible at this point in her life. She almost felt like a teenager. Just the thought of Morgan touching her thrilled Grace and brought her back to her teens. He gently stroked her hair, and then whispered in her ear, "Grace, you are so beautiful."

She started to worry that the kids would come in and see them. But when Morgan gently put his arms around her waist and drew her close to him, it was as if she didn't have a care in the world and no one else existed. Then he kissed her. His kiss was slow and thoughtful. Standing on her tiptoes, she pushed herself up. Morgan, like a prince, lifted her toward him. He was so damn sexy, and she wanted him so much. If the kids hadn't been there, she would have undressed him in a matter of seconds. Still, she was a grandmother who baked cookies and made lunch, not the sex goddess Morgan had created.

"That was by far the best kiss I've ever had," she said. "Why don't you help me get the kids to bed, and we can do the same."

Morgan couldn't resist that offer. "Not a problem. I haven't spent much time with children lately, but I can learn."

Grace laughed. "Like how you hadn't kissed anyone like that in a while?"

"I'm a quick learner. Watch me."

Chapter Nine

Jack and Victoria got their marriage license, which wasn't exactly a difficult chore in Vegas. They were ready to take the deep plunge. Jack had hired a driver for the night, but he couldn't help but miss Morgan. He wished his friend could have been with him on such an important day.

Morgan was so much more than a driver to Jack. Even though Morgan's proper mindset never allowed for too much closeness on his part, he always stepped up to the plate like a parent would. He was always nearby, and kept Jack on a straight path. Even though Jack's mother loved him, she was very social and loved traveling. While he wished she had been home more, Morgan made sure Jack became a respectable person.

Planning a wedding in a matter of hours was not something Jack could have ever foreseen, but he was determined to marry Victoria. Some marriages began and ended in a matter of days, but Jack always saw marriage as a serious commitment.

He had never been in love, at least not the kind of love that mattered. He was always afraid that he wouldn't know the real thing when it happened, but actually knowing all those other women made it easy to see that Victoria was the right one. "Love" was a word Jack rarely used, and he didn't doubt he was doing something crazy, but he was up for the challenge.

Victoria laid her head back, trying to get a catnap on the way to the "chapel of love," as she called it. She loved being able to close her eyes for short periods of time to recharge her battery, which was her way of coping with being busy and not having enough time to sleep.

She was happy, but also very nervous about having a new man in her life. She liked the thought of having Jack with her. It wasn't only his good looks. What really mattered was that Victoria could talk to him. In all the years she was married to Michael, he never really listened to her. Jack listened.

It was close to nine when the driver pulled up to the chapel. Jack had made all the plans; that was something Victoria could get used to. After many years of doing things on her own, it was a pleasant change just to sit back and be surprised. Michael had never been around much; he spent most of his time at off-track betting or schmoozing with his gambling buddies at bars. He didn't think she knew, but Victoria had hired an investigator when she started suspecting something was going wrong. She didn't like having to spy on him, and neither did her sister. Ava always argued in Michael's favor. Sometimes,

Victoria thought Ava was the one who should have married Michael. She was much more accepting of his faults.

Victoria knew she had a habit of overthinking things. She had seen so many movies where actors fell in love and got married so fast they didn't know what hit them. This was reality, and she wasn't an actress playing a part. She had kids, a practice, and an ex—who undoubtedly would think she was crazy to be doing this.

While they were waiting, Jack noticed Victoria's deep breathing. "You know we don't have to do this right now," he said. "I don't want you to do something that might not be right for you. I'm hoping this is going to be forever. Is that what's scaring you?"

Victoria shook her head. She was keeping her answers to gestures, rather than words.

"Let's not do this," Jack said. "I'm sorry. Maybe I came on too strong. I just want to be with you."

"I guess you know about how people react to things that scare them," she said, trying to minimize her deep breathing and pounding heartbeat.

Jack held onto her tightly. "I can tell when it's too much to handle. I've fallen in love with you, but I can wait. I don't need a piece of paper to know you're the one. I think what we have is so good it can't be broken. We will work everything out because we love each other. I know it's fast, but sometimes love happens that way. It doesn't have to be overwhelming."

"It's my kids. I want to be with you because I love you, but I also love my children. I worry about how they will handle this. This is going to be tough, and I'm not sure a ready-made family is such a good thing for you."

"I've met them all. Been there, done that. We can do this. It might not be easy at first, but we will transition. In no time at all, we'll be happy."

She smiled and felt a lot better. She really liked how safe she felt with him. Victoria had been living her life, helping everyone and working all the time. She never stopped to think that she needed someone. It felt good to be held. Jack was a good man, and she wasn't going to let him go.

Victoria straightened her lace shirt, pushed her hair out of her face, and was ready to go.

"You want to know something?" she said. "Just for the record, this chapel is beautiful. I love the red roses leading the way inside. I think this is going to be a great night to remember when we're old and gray. Everything looks so wonderful, and the music is charming. There is one thing. Do you think they have a rabbi on call?"

"When we get home, we can have a rabbi re-marry us," Jack said. "How does that sound?"

"Perfect. Also, do you think we can keep this a secret for a little while?"

"Yes, if that's what you want." He took Victoria's hand and kissed it. "I'm in love with you. As crazy as this seems, this is going to be good. If you want to wait to tell everyone, I can do that. As long as we know we love each other."

"I know that. This is the craziest thing I've ever done."

"Sometimes in life, crazy is the only way to go. Safe is fine, but never trying new things can be bad for the soul. That's not me talking; it's what one of my professors told me when I wanted to quit school. I wanted to do anything but give advice, because I was afraid I wouldn't be able to help others. It took me a long time—and a lot of hard work—before I could really express myself. I think I accomplished that in my own way."

Tears fell from Victoria's eyes. "I can see why your patients and your readers love you. I love you. I can't believe that Andrew running into you could change my life in such a good way. It's so fast for me, but it feels right."

"Me too, but I've been waiting my whole life to feel the way I feel when I look at you. From the moment I laid my eyes on you, I knew you were the one I had been waiting for."

Victoria took his hand. "Come on, let's go. We have a wedding to attend. Do you think we can break a glass? I love tradition."

Jack reached under the seat and took out a box. He opened it, and there was a goblet. "My first wedding gift to you. We will break the glass and have years of happiness. I can learn to like tradition."

Both of them walked into the chapel, knowing they were doing the right thing.

Chapter Ten

Ava was glad she came to Vegas. She decided long ago that if she didn't have the man she wanted, she didn't want anyone. Michael had been through a lot, but even though he was the one causing problems for her sister, he was still a good man in Ava's eyes.

She saw Michael looking out at the tables in the casino, but she wasn't going to let him do anything stupid. Not on her watch. "Listen, before you leave for Chicago, let's do something fun," she said. "You remember what that is, don't you?"

He looked as if she was crazy to think he would go anywhere with her. The two of them had not always been on the best of terms, but Michael was down on himself, so he listened. He didn't really want to go back to Chicago alone, but he also didn't feel like being rejected and then going home to his shitty existence.

"We can go anywhere you want," Ava continued. "I have vacation time. A month or two, or whatever you need. Let's just go and have a good time. We will worry when we get back. For now, let's enjoy life."

"Will that make it better?"

"I think it will. Sometimes the mind clears in different surroundings, and whatever wasn't working will either work or it won't. Haven't you ever heard about freeing the mind from clutter?"

"Are you kidding me?"

"Have you ever wondered why we argue so much?" She was a bit sarcastic, but in her mind she had wanted to say a lot more. She had decided to turn over a new leaf by being a little bit more caring. Hopefully she had it in her.

Michael stopped at a bench and asked her to sit with him. She did so reluctantly, not wanting to hear what he was probably going to say. "There are some things we probably should have said years ago," he began, "but now seems like a good time."

She nodded, waiting for the shoe to drop. She deserved it for the way she broke up with him years ago—not that they were serious, but she did sleep with him. Michael was her first real love, but she didn't know it until he was gone. By then, there was nothing she could do but put up a wall and be available when Victoria had enough. She just didn't think it would take so many years.

"Look, Ava, I wouldn't have brought this up, but you started. You and I are worlds apart. We don't think alike or have anything in common. Oh, and by the way, everything you say usually infuriates the hell out of me. You've been a complete ass to me and never apologized for throwing me to the wind. Not that Victoria was the wind, but you never even said you were sorry."

"Well, maybe I am sorry."

"Oh, and you could have been a little nicer to Victoria, especially at the end of our marriage. She probably needed her sister. She's always been there for you. And, let me add, you sometimes don't even look at me when I'm talking to you. Like now. You're pissing me off."

Ava wasn't surprised by his candor, but she wasn't happy with it either. "Are you done?"

"Yes, for now."

"Okay, I guess I deserved that. Let me say one thing, and for the rest of the night we can forget about this wonderful, heart-warming discussion. The reason I treated you badly was because I loved you, and I always have.

After we broke it off and you started dating my sister, I knew I made a mistake, but it was too late. So there it is. I'm sorry, really sorry. Now can we get on with our lives and forget about apologies? I don't love apologizing."

"You didn't just break it off. You stood me up more than once, slept with a couple of my friends—who are no longer my friends—and you never looked back."

"Okay, now we need a truce. Let's not keep going back, but let me add just one thing. You never acted like you cared, and you were a shit. Now let's forget about what I did and move forward."

Ava, ever the free spirit, put her arms around his neck and whispered in his ear. "Don't take this the wrong way, but tonight is going to be one of the best nights of your life." Then she kissed him with everything she had, and he liked it, so he kissed her back. They looked at each other, shocked by the emotional impact of just one kiss.

"I'm not Victoria," Ava said. "I make mistakes and then I move on. I'm not asking you to change. I'm just asking you on a date, not a marriage proposal."

Michael laughed. "Like that's happening."

Then she kissed him again, and this time it lasted a lot longer. It didn't take much time to get back to Ava's room and get reacquainted with each other. Strange as it seemed, they felt comfortable with each other even after years of separation.

Later that evening, they decided to go out and have fun—no rules, no time limit, just the whole night to do whatever they felt like doing. They were both champions at having fun and drinking too much. They landed at a karaoke bar, and then at a casino. That was the last place Michael should have been. Sobering up, Ava realized Michael was standing at a roulette table, cheering.

Ava jumped up and ran over to Michael. Her heart was racing. "Shit, what are you doing? Don't do this. Please. I don't want to be the one to push you off the ledge."

"Actually, I'm feeling pretty good. Victoria keeps telling me to make a new life, and I think I may just do that. Are you here because you feel sorry for me, or are you here because you want to be?"

Ava took his hand and they left the casino. Michael wasn't sure he understood his feelings, because he rarely let himself think of a future, but he was very happy at that moment. "It's not the booze talking; it's me," he said. "I have to confess that I'm actually enjoying myself. It's been a very long time since I felt anything other than sad. Thank you for tonight."

"You're thanking me? Where did Michael Feingold go, and who is this man talking to me?"

"It's me. I've had a great time tonight. You have helped so much. I can't explain how great it feels to be with someone who doesn't hate everything I do."

"Michael, did you hear me tonight? I love you. I always have." And then she kissed him.

"Ava, you sure know how to have a party. Let's keep this going. I'm feeling so good right now."

"Me too," she added, grabbing onto his arm. "Now what?"

By a twist of fate, they were standing outside a small chapel. Michael looked at her. "What do you think? Should we get married?"

"Are you serious? Married? I would think that would be the furthest thing from your mind."

"Do you like being alone, Ava?"

"No, I hate it, but I'm not alone when I'm with Victoria and the kids. That's why I stay there, even though my mother thinks it's because I have nowhere else to go. There were other offers. Not ones that matched the feelings I still had for you, but there were offers."

Michael took her hand and led her inside the chapel. "We can't tell Victoria. Not yet. Right now, it's just you and me, and no one has to know anything until we decide the time is right."

She said yes, but she couldn't guarantee it would stay that way. Ava had been known to break a promise or two, and to sometimes say too much too soon, and Michael had the same problem.

Twenty minutes later, they were married.

Chapter Eleven

Victoria took a long, hot shower before she ate the gourmet breakfast Jack had sent up. He was out playing golf, and probably talking to anyone who knew him, which could be just about everyone.

He was so entertaining that she wished he was the one giving the speech. However, it was going to be her, so she needed to pull herself together and write a good presentation. She was unprepared, which was not like her. Really, she thought, nothing she had done since getting on the plane for Vegas was like her.

She ate the cold eggs and overbuttered toast, which was how she always ate her breakfast. She was usually running late, and sometimes ate on the way to the office. It usually wasn't very good by then, but it did the trick. If she didn't have time for lunch, at least she had something in her stomach.

In the meantime, Jack had also sent up a dozen white roses and a box of chocolates, which was so romantic. Victoria wasn't used to this treatment, but it was fun. She didn't get to have a honeymoon when she married

Michael; she still had finals to finish. They had planned to take a vacation later that year, but that was out of the question once she found out she was pregnant. As the years passed, there was never a right time to go away, and money was tight. That never changed in the twelve years they were married.

Looking at her wardrobe, Victoria reminded herself that she never brought the shoes back to the boutique. She quickly called and asked for Monique, but learned she was off for the day. Victoria figured she would just drop off the shoes when she went down to get something to wear.

Her thoughts were interrupted by a loud knock, and then another. Her first instinct was not to answer, but the recurring knocks told her they weren't going away. She quickly cleaned up by throwing everything in her suitcase, then answered.

Her mother and the three kids were standing there. They had balloons, and started singing "Happy Birthday" as soon as she opened the door. Victoria thought it was really nice, if she didn't have a secret that could blow up and cause all sorts of confusion.

"Kids, turn on the TV," Grace said. "Your mother and I are stepping outside for a moment." She smiled, but Victoria knew that smile was not for her. Once they were alone in the hall, Grace continued. "What is going on here, and where are your sister and Michael?"

"Is Ava here? I haven't seen her, but why is she here?"

"She wanted to come and surprise you, so she left after your plane took off."

"Who's with Angus? You didn't send him to the Party Motel, did you?"

"No, he's at the Vet Villa on Michigan Avenue. Not to worry, I got him first-class treatment and told them to order from Mally's. He loves their hamburgers."

"Fine. I hope he's okay."

"Believe me, he's fine. There won't be any more surprises."

"Well, there have been plenty of surprises over these last couple of days. And I love you for trying, but I have to finish writing my speech. Just making some changes." She lied, but it was better than telling her mother she had gotten married instead of writing. "Be a great mom and take the kids for breakfast."

Grace gave her a look. "You've always been a terrible liar. I know you're hiding something. Or someone. Did you sleep with Michael?"

"What are you thinking? That wouldn't happen if he were the last man in the world. I don't want to be rude, and it was so nice of you to come, but can we do this later?"

"We can. I'm going to be listening to you today. How terrific is that?"

"It's not open to the public."

"I'm not the public. I'm your mother. Besides, I know the right people."

• • •

Victoria was glad she was only scheduled to speak once, and doubted she would ever stand on a stage again. The good news was that after this convention she would own her house free and clear, and speaking to crowds was going to be a memory.

When she looked at the audience, she saw her mother was there waiting for her to be brilliant, but that wasn't going to happen. This was going to be tough, but she had been through rougher times.

A few minutes into her presentation, Victoria's mind started to wander. She thought about how horrible she looked, and made a deal with herself to throw out her old clothes the minute she got home. Realizing how petty she had become, she snapped out of it. She stayed on topic and talked about how she considered a good bedside manner one of the most important ways to keep patients.

"Mothers and fathers are usually very nervous when they have to bring their children in for a sick checkup," Victoria said. "They are thinking about 'what if?' So you have to take their feelings into consideration. Sometimes I write down instructions, because parents may forget things when they leave the office. After all, being a parent isn't an easy job."

Looking out at the audience, Victoria realized she was boring. She knew she was a very good doctor, but public speaking was not her specialty. One thing she prided herself on was her ability to admit her faults. She was also a quick thinker. At that moment, she had an idea, one that would have everyone in the audience on their feet with applause.

"I wanted to thank everyone for being here today," she said. "Before I end today's program, I have a surprise for you. In our audience is a successful doctor who is known for his wonderful books, Dr. Jack Winston." She looked right into his eyes and smiled. "We're so lucky to have him here today. He knows everything about raising children the right way, so let's see what he has to say. Jack, please come up."

Victoria knew she did the right thing, because the polite audience suddenly become a rather noisy, happy group. The thunderous applause didn't stop until Jack was standing before them—and even then, it took several minutes to quiet everyone down. She was thrilled.

"Well, it's good to hear the roar of hands clapping," Victoria continued. "As long as we have Jack with us, let's open the room to questions. If that's okay with the good doctor."

Jack nodded, but it was his smile that signaled to her that he was okay with her plan.

Victoria took a seat next to her mother, feeling elated to be off that stage.

"Great idea, honey; you're back in my good graces," Grace joked. "Where were you last night? Apparently not writing your speech. And what happened to Michael? He took off like a bat out of hell right after you pulled away in the cab. He's not answering his cell. Is he here?"

"He was here, and I asked him to go home. But if I know Michael, he's still here."

Grace stopped the questions as she listened to Jack, who was certainly getting audience participation.

It was easy for Jack. He never needed notes; he just opened his mouth and the words came out. "It's so nice to be here among my peers. It's been awhile since I've been to a convention packed with such esteemed doctors. Thank you, Doctor Hudson, for such a generous action. I like to talk, and hopefully everyone will listen." Again, the audience responded with applause.

Jack belonged at the podium. He looked good standing there, smiling and owning the room. His profile was strong and rigid, and his eyes focused directly on his audience. Victoria knew she would never have what it took to put an audience at ease the way Jack did. Everyone was listening to his every word. He was incredibly good, and she began to understand why he was constantly on the bestseller list and overbooked with public appearances. Just his smile was worth millions. She loved him, and she barely knew him.

"Okay, where shall we begin?" Jack couldn't seem to take his eyes off Victoria, but he knew he had to perform.

Victoria watched her mother become instantly happy. "Where are the kids?" she asked.

"They're fine. Shh. I'm listening."

"Grace, where are they?" She always called her mother by her first name when she was uneasy about something.

"They're with your sister. Now, can I please listen to the man who hasn't taken his eyes off you for a second? I'm not stupid, dear. I know something happened. But we can talk about that later."

Jack acknowledged one of the doctors sitting in the audience, who had trained with him. "Jenny Albright, how nice to see you. What's your question?"

"Jack, as you know, we lead very busy lives," she began. "I have four children, who I love to pieces, but…"

Jack laughed right along with the audience. "You've been busy, my old friend, since we've last seen each other."

"I have indeed. My question is, I manage my office, attend conventions, and do a lot of in- patient consults every month. So why in hell can't I manage my children's behavior? Sometimes they just go wild, and it's usually when I can barely keep my eyes open."

"Jenny, your kids know when you're tired. But, get this—they don't care. They haven't seen you all day, and they want you to be there for them. Sounds simple, but it takes some work."

"How, Jack? I could use all the advice I can get. How do I make the time to be a good mother and a good physician?"

"At least once a week, go home early. Take the kids out to dinner and turn off your cell phone. Look at them. Really look at them. They need you, and believe me, you need them. Talk to them about their day, one at a time. I know leaving early is a radical thought for a doctor, but even doctors need to unwind."

"True," she answered back, while the others clapped loudly. "Do you take time to unwind?"

"I try, but it's not that easy. Remember, just because I give advice doesn't mean I can take it." The audience roared with laughter, and Jack seemed very happy to know he had them. "When you're on your deathbed, your last thought will not be, 'Thank you God for allowing me to work twenty-four-seven.'"

Jenny nodded. "I'll try. Promise. Is all this in your book?"

"Similar examples."

"Then I'll buy it."

Jack handed her a copy. "I seem to have a few in my bag."

Chapter Twelve

The conference was over, but everyone seemed to enjoy Jack. He was the life of the party. He made people laugh, and gave great advice at the same time.

While Grace was watching the speech, Morgan made sure everything was perfect for Victoria's birthday. He came with Grace—in fact, he insisted he wanted to be there for her. She was really happy about that. Strange as it seemed, she had fallen for him.

Grace had been with a few different men since her husband died, but she had never been with anyone like Morgan. She wondered why some woman hadn't snatched him up. He was a good catch. Not only was he charming and very attentive, but he was a good cook and made the bed. Grace had already slept with him, since pregnancy wasn't a worry for her.

It was always difficult for Grace to plan things when her girls had their own agendas, and this party was another example. It seemed as if Ava had disappeared along with Michael. Grace didn't know what to make of that. The two of them usually fought like cats and dogs, but she hoped they might try to get along in different surroundings, at least for the day. Michael had brought the children back after the conference was over, and then left while the rest of them went to dinner.

The casino had a side room available for private parties. It seemed like a good place for a birthday if there wasn't going to be drama, but getting the family around a table to eat was grounds for trouble in paradise. When Jack walked in and saw Morgan, he did a double take. "What are you doing here?" he asked

Morgan pulled Jack off to the side. "Jack, I'm in love with Grace. Don't say another word. It just happened."

At first, Jack didn't say anything, but once the shock wore off he couldn't help himself. "You're in love. In a minute? To a woman you barely know? How is this possible?"

"For the same reason you hopped on a plane to be with a woman you met outside of a book signing. Need I say more?"

Jack knew he was right. So far, this whole adventure with Victoria seemed exhilarating. Victoria and her family seemed to live a lifestyle completely opposite to the one Jack had been living for the last thirty years, but that's what made it so exciting. He had taken a gamble, and he happened to be in the right place for that.

"You're lucky your mother isn't here," Morgan said. "She'd love it if you started dating a woman with three kids."

Jack laughed, thinking of what his mother had said when he called her that morning. It wasn't exactly what she said, but what she did—she dropped the phone and called for her loving live-in boyfriend, who was only ten years younger. "Sam, come quick. My Jack found his princess, and she has three kids. I'm a grandmother! It's about time." Sophie Winston Wainwright was a little upset when she found out she couldn't send gifts, but she thought it would be better if she waited until she met the children.

When he and Morgan were done talking, Jack sat next to Victoria, holding her hand and letting her know he was there for her. She took a deep breath and looked around. The kids ran over to Victoria and surrounded her with balloons, shouting, "Happy birthday, Mommy! Happy, happy, happy birthday!"

Jack was smiling, despite being nervous around kids. Even though he wrote about kids, he never knew what to expect because he hadn't had many opportunities to be around them. According to his old rules, he would never date anyone with children. Well, he definitely broke that rule.

When she sensed Jack's awkwardness around her kids, Victoria silently began to question everything that had happened in the last twenty-four hours. He seemed to be trying, but she didn't feel comfortable watching him try so hard. He was a little stiff, and understandably so, but she still hoped for an easier transition.

"Jack, meet my kids again," she said. "Allyson, Noah, and Andrew. I know you've met them before."

Andrew hugged Jack, and Jack actually hugged him back. However, Andrew had just eaten a sucker, and Victoria hadn't had a chance to wipe his hands. Jack's Armani jacket was now sticky, and there were several stains on his shoulder. There were also signs of punch on his pants, but they were down by his ankle, so Victoria hoped he wouldn't notice.

Victoria reached for Andrew's sticky hands, and cleaned them with a wet wipe. "Sorry, Jack," she said. "He's usually not that messy."

"Not a problem," he said. "I didn't like this jacket any-way." That was pretty far from the truth. He loved the jacket, and it was actually the first time he had ever worn it.

Finally, Ava showed up—with Michael right behind her. Grace sensed something bizarre was going on, but she didn't yet have the time to put the pieces of the puzzle together. Shortly thereafter, she noticed Victoria motion-ing for Ava to meet her in the ladies' room.

This was where Grace's mothering skills came into play. She always tried to be subtle, but that wasn't her strong suit. She inched toward Ava. "What's going on?" she asked. "I saw Michael right behind you when you came in, and something's up. You didn't sleep with him, did you?"

Ava angrily looked at her mother. "Did you just ask me what I thought you did? Why in hell would you think that? I just walked in ahead of him. Is that a crime, or something really suspicious? Really, mother."

"What if your sister saw you?"

"What if she did? He's leaving soon, and they're not married anymore. Mom, don't worry so much about Victoria. She's a big girl."

"It's a mother's job to worry."

"Well, you need to stop. You need to focus on you. I have a great idea, Mom. Get yourself a boyfriend so you can think about something other than us. We're fine, just different. It might be rough sailing sometimes, but she's my sister. Like it or not, she's stuck with me, and I'm stuck with her."

"What if I did have a boyfriend? Aren't mothers allowed to have sex?"

"Oh boy. You had sex with Morgan?"

"And if I did?"

Ava couldn't believe this was her mother talking. "Hold on, you're not telling? Maybe you shouldn't. This isn't something I need to know."

"That's ridiculous. You're a big girl. You can handle knowing your mother had sex."

"Never mind. Sorry." Ava noticed her mother winking at Morgan as they talked. She knew right then that she was right. "Not that this chat wasn't a good one, Mother, but I've got to go. Victoria's waiting."

"Maybe I should come too."

"No, not a good idea. You know Victoria. If there isn't a problem now, wait a minute and she'll find one. I love her, but she's so busy trying to be perfect that she never enjoys the moment. She should do something outlandish for a change. That would make her more human."

Grace sighed, hoping there wouldn't be any drama, but she knew something was brewing. She used to be able to control her girls, but she had little—if any—clout as they grew up.

However, this time it might have been her fault. She did send Michael to Vegas, even though she immediately questioned herself about that. She still loved him despite everything he had done, and part of her liked the idea that Victoria and Michael might get back together. Stranger things had happened.

She rarely took sides between her girls, but she knew Victoria had a much better understanding of life than Ava did. Ava loved the wild side—even if there wasn't an edge, she found it. Victoria was pliable, while Ava was always non-negotiable. She knew her children, but a pro-active mother knew when to bow out, and Grace decided she would do just that.

No one except Victoria was in the ladies' room when Ava pranced in. "What took so long?" Victoria asked, as she pretended to primp in the mirror.

Ava thought her sister could use more primping, but Victoria was beautiful even without makeup. Besides, Ava wasn't one to give beauty advice, since she often ran around with her hair pulled up by combs, wearing an oversized sweatshirt with a hood pulled up so that only her eyes showed. "Our mother wanted to know if I slept with Michael," Ava answered.

"Has she gone mad? Why would he do that?"

Ava didn't know quite how to take that. She took a second look at her sister and realized there was something just a little different about her. She had that love glow. "Victoria, you look really good today. You must have gotten a lot of sleep last night—or a lot of sex."

"As a matter of fact, I didn't sleep at all."

"Really?" Suddenly, Ava was interested. "Go on."

"Give me a minute. I need to figure out how to tell you this."

"Just fucking tell me. I'm not shy."

"I took a ride on the wild side. And it actually felt good."

Ava knew it must be something wicked. "Okay, let's hear it. I know something's not kosher in the cabinet if you picked me to confide in. My standards are a little tarnished, but that's what makes life fun. So give me the scoop, and you'd better be fast. Otherwise, Grace will figure out something is going on, and I doubt you want her in this conversation. She's busy with her boyfriend, Morgan. She slept with him."

Victoria laughed. "You're kidding, right?"

"Don't think it was a joke."

"Grace doesn't joke or interfere, but we know she loves to be in on everything. How silly of her to think you and Michael were sleeping together. The chances of that are slim to none."

Ava started pacing back and forth, trying to figure out how this was all going to go down. She didn't know how to tell her sister she slept with Michael—but it was getting easier by the minute, because her sister was starting to piss her off. Nothing good ever came of that.

Suddenly, Victoria blurted it out. "If I don't tell anyone soon, I will burst. I got married last night."

Ava just stood there, looking at her sister. "And I thought I had a strange night. Who the hell did you marry?" When she turned to look at her sister, she knew. "Oh my God. You can't be serious. You married the psychiatrist. Holy shit."

"I did. I married Jack Winston. We're keeping it a secret for a while. I'm not sure how the kids and Michael will take it, and I don't know how Mom would feel about me doing this whole thing so fast. I know she loves Michael, and wanted us to get back together, but that will never happen."

"I think a new man in your life is good, but you don't really know him. He could be a sex freak, or something like that." Ava looked at her sister, trying to figure out what Victoria might say to her situation. "I also have some Vegas news."

"I doubt you can top mine."

"Well, here goes. I might be able to top yours, but you need to sit down."

"Go ahead. I'm listening."

"I got married last night, too. And we decided to keep it a secret for a similar reason."

"What the hell? You picked someone up last night and married him? Why would you do that?"

"Because I love him. And for the record, Michael will be fine with your news. I married him last night in a small chapel on the strip. He finally got it right. I can make him happy."

Victoria wasn't sure if she should laugh or cry. "Have you lost it? You married my husband."

"Actually, you're divorced. And so is he."

"How did that happen? Was he drunk? He must have been drunk."

"Hell no. He finally realized he married the wrong girl. You never did understand him, but he's perfect for me. I don't care about the bad things he did. I can help him. Don't take this the wrong way, but you didn't have time to help him. I do."

"So you're saying all of his problems were my fault? I was the gambler who blew everything and almost lost our house? If you remember, you were the one who told me to watch him because he was hanging out in bars and at the track. Knowing all of that, you still want him. Are you crazy?"

"No, not crazy, just in love. Always have been. Isn't one at a time enough for you?" Victoria started to walk out, but Ava stopped her. "We need to talk about this before you go out and make a fool of yourself."

"Are you kidding me? You married my ex and I'm the fool? I thought you hated him."

"I had to. He was your husband. I have always loved him. I couldn't tell you that, could I?"

Victoria was getting angrier by the minute. "You were screwing him in my house, weren't you?"

Ava didn't say anything else; if she did, they would never talk again. Now she was really pissed. There certainly weren't any congratulatory remarks for either of them. They both stormed out of the ladies' room, fast and furious. They hoped their mother wasn't watching, but she was. Grace knew there was another war to contend with, but she would take care of it later. Right now, they were celebrating.

"Now that everyone is here, let's sing 'Happy Birthday' to Victoria," she said. Like soldiers, everyone did what they were told and sang, but the war would go on until someone waved the white flag.

Morgan was watching in awe at how Grace handled her family. He was trying to figure out a way to get her alone, so they could spend the rest of the day together.

It wasn't as hard as he thought, since she whispered in his ear, "What does a girl have to do to get a drink around here?" She loved that line. She once heard it on TV, and finally had the right guy to use it on.

Just as Grace had watched her daughters, they were watching her. Victoria hadn't met Morgan, but from the way things looked, she thought she should. Hearing her mother slept with him was a little shocking, but she knew there had been others, even though her mother didn't think she knew.

"I guess I'm the only one who hasn't met you," Victoria said.

Morgan laughed. "I feel like I already know you. Your mother kind of likes you."

Victoria laughed. "She's my greatest fan, and I love it, but let's not tell her I said so. She's the one who pushed me to go to medical school. I owe her everything."

Morgan and Victoria seemed to be getting along nicely, as far as Jack could tell. What seemed interesting to him was how a small family like this shared a lot of problems, but everyone cared about each other even when they disagreed. It was comforting to watch. He could take lessons from them. He didn't know where to begin, but marrying into this family was a start.

Grace believed in the idea of "till death do us part," and she followed that right up until the end of her husband's life. At first, she had a wonderful marriage to a great guy, but she was very young when she met Maurice and fell for his charm. He was several years older, but that didn't matter to her. She married him after dating for two and half weeks, and she loved him every day they spent together—but that didn't mean she was always happy.

How could any woman be happy when her husband was having a longtime affair with a woman from work? He was a lawyer, and she was an associate. Grace knew for some time, but she was very busy with her kids. So for the better part of their lives, she shared her husband with someone else.

Maurice's longtime girlfriend came up to Grace at the chapel where his funeral services were held, and apologized for the years she took from her. Grace, being generous, hugged her and said, "He was a wonderful man who had time for both of us. We're both left, so have a good life with however how many years we have left. If you find another man, don't waste time waiting. Go for it." That was what Grace intended to do now with Morgan.

Three hours before they headed back to Chicago, Grace married Morgan, and she wasn't one bit afraid about her future. Morgan was the man she had been waiting for her entire life, and she knew it. He had her the moment he lifted her up and told her he wanted to hold her in his arms for the rest of her life. Now Grace had a secret, just like her daughters.

Chapter Thirteen

After Ava told Michael about her argument with Victoria, she decided not to fly back with her family. She made up an excuse about having to check out a new hotel, hoping she and Michael could have a few days together.

Just as she waved goodbye to her family as they boarded the plane, she got a text from Michael. "Meet me at the American Airlines coffee bar." Ava was so excited she could barely breathe.

She felt lucky, as if she had won a jackpot, though her sister obviously thought differently. This was more than just a fight; her rift with Victoria could be permanent. Ava felt terrible that, after all the fights that came and went, this one might not.

Michael was waiting for her, coffee in hand. "Got you one. Black, three sugars, and a splash of milk, right?" To her, it was a big deal that he remembered.

She hugged him firmly, but his hug felt distant. It wasn't like it should have been after a wonderful night of lovemaking. "Okay, what's going on?"

Michael took her hand and led her to a table. "We need to talk about what we did. Let's sit. Ava, you know damn well we shouldn't have done this. We weren't thinking, and our passion took over."

"I guess Victoria called you. I'm not surprised by what you're saying. Maybe she was right. You would have to be drunk to be with me."

"That's not true at all. You're a beautiful woman. She shouldn't have said that."

"But she did, and it hurt. I may be tough, but I do have feelings."

"We both had a lot to drink, and we did something spontaneous without a backup plan. We never thought of how this could hurt the people we love. How are the kids going to understand any of this? You're their aunt."

"I love those kids just as if they were my own. I don't want to hurt them either."

"You know, Ava, I'm not exactly great husband material, as you stated many a time."

"Can't argue with that."

"I want to be ready to do what's necessary when I start a new life. For starters, I have to work."

Ava was quiet for a few minutes, trying to compose herself without saying something she would regret. "Kids get over things faster than adults do. They don't delve; they try to go with the flow. We can make them understand. They love both of us, and they love their mother. This can work."

"I've never been the responsible one, but now I need to be. I can't believe Victoria did something that stupid, marrying a guy she barely knows. Jack was a great guy in college, from what I remember, and he's apparently respected in his field, but who does this? What could she have been thinking?"

Shockingly, Ava found herself defending her sister. "Maybe, for the first time in her life, she didn't think."

"I'm not really judging her," Michael said. "Well, maybe I am. Victoria is always thinking."

"Victoria's a woman who's been hurt so badly by you that she's not seeing things clearly. You know how she is. Victoria is the one who checks everything out, who plays it safe. Don't tell her I said so, but she's also the one who's there for all of us. She might think I'm selfish and ungrateful, but that's not true."

"So you agree we went too fast?"

"As much as I hate to admit it, you might be right. We can't undo what she did, but we don't have to add fuel to the fire. It's about the kids. Maybe they aren't ready for both of you to be married to different people. I don't even understand exactly how this went down."

"I'm not sorry about what happened last night. I don't want to end us."

Ava was surprised. "You don't? I thought that's where this conversation was going."

"It felt great to be with someone who cared about me and wasn't always finding fault with every last thing I do."

"You did do some really bad things, but you're human, and I think you've changed. Everyone deserves a second chance."

"We just have to be adult about all of this. I might have changed a little, but I need more work. You know that."

"Agreed. So what's going to be the next step?"

"When I get myself together, we will both tell the kids what happened. They will be happy if we are. It might take a little while, but we have the rest of our lives to be together."

Ava had never thought they had a chance, but now they did. Michael wasn't sorry he married her, and she didn't care how long she had to wait to tell everyone.

Michael smiled and kissed her forehead before heading out. "I will be fine. I'll leave today. What about you?"

"I'll stay a day or two and then get back. I know my sister, and a few days apart will do us both a world of good."

Ava held him for a few minutes. She could feel his body quiver. It had seemed as if his nerves were a little frayed. "I'm here for you," she said. "I've been waiting twelve years, so I think I can wait a little longer. I think you know I get you, and that has to count for something."

"It counts for everything."

Ava kissed him so passionately that he almost fell over. "Michael, no matter what you do, it will not change how much I love you, and how much I have always loved you."

She sat there for a long while after Michael left. It was just a trip to Vegas, but somehow her whole life had changed in a day, and now she was sure things were looking up.

• • •

Ava cried all the way back to the hotel, partly from joy and partly from sadness. Her cab driver was speeding through all the intersections. He couldn't stand the crying, but he could still hear it even with music playing in his ear.

The cabbie leaned his head back. "Missy, are you okay? Whoever the asshole is, forget him. Men are a dime a dozen."

Ava stopped crying long enough to answer. "You got that shit right."

"Do you want to stop for a drink?" he asked. "My treat."

"Don't think so. You could be a killer for all I know."

"Missy, killer cab drivers don't stop for drinks. They just drive you to the forest preserve."

"That sounds reassuring."

"I have six children at home, a wife, a mother-in-law, a dog, two cats, and my brother, who just appeared one day with no money and no job."

Ava couldn't help but laugh. She stopped crying, realizing it seemed as if she was whining, and she hated women who did that. "Why don't you let me by you a drink? You need it more than I do—your family sounds like mine, but worse. Maybe what they say is true, that misery likes company. Stop the car and let's have a drink."

For some reason, Ava liked to do things other people never would, such as stopping for a drink with someone she didn't know and might never see again. It made her feel powerful. When the cabbie had a few too many drinks, she left him at the bar and took another cab home. She wasn't that stupid.

After three days of staying with friends who couldn't wait for her to leave, Ava made the journey back home. She didn't have any other place to go, and she wasn't the best houseguest. Besides, she needed her laundry done.

Chapter Fourteen

Secrets eventually surface, and a family can become more divided the longer a secret is withheld. Grace and her daughters were as close as any family could be—until each of them decided not to come clean.

For Victoria and Jack, the decision to wait to tell the kids—and their friends and family—about their marriage had become harder than they imagined, and it appeared that their honeymoon was over before it began. They had to live separately, though they met for an occasional lunch, a few dinners, and a lot of late-night hotel visits—which were steamy, but way too short. With their busy schedules, that was the only way for them to share any time at all.

Victoria had never been to Jack's apartment, but it seemed like the logical place to go after they'd visited every hotel on Michigan Avenue. Victoria nervously stood outside of Jack's apartment, trying to calm herself. He lived in luxury, while she had spent years worrying that she might not be able to keep up with her mortgage payments and would eventually lose her house.

She had postponed going to Jack's, but it was time. She had a feeling Jack's apartment was something right out of a beautiful magazine, so she wasn't the least bit surprised that she had to check in with the doorman before going up. She wouldn't have been shocked if he had made her open her purse and let him look inside, just like airport security. But as she was signing in, Jack was coming from the elevator.

His hello kiss was so warm and friendly, Victoria decided to leave all her internal baggage at the door and move on. However, the doorman was still looking her over, with a superior attitude on his young face.

"Randolph," Jack said, "meet Victoria, my wife—but that's not for publication or idle chitchat. We would like some privacy."

Randolph now realized his sizing her up might have given Victoria the wrong idea. He shook her hand. "So very nice to meet you, Victoria. My lips are sealed."

"How nice to meet you, Randolph. I look forward to seeing you again." She really wasn't planning to come back often, but it sounded good. She couldn't see her children living there, and she was certain the other residents were unlikely to welcome her crew.

Jack laughed, knowing he couldn't wait to tell the neighbors. At one time or another, several of them had tried to set him up and get him married off, but none of the lovely ladies they suggested was right for him.

The elevator came and, once they were inside, Jack quickly closed the door behind them and hit the stop button. Victoria laughed, knowing that Jack was planning something. She couldn't help but feel like she was in a movie. It was kind of fun, so different from any life she had ever known.

"Jack, you're kidding, right? Stopping the elevator?"

"Nope, not kidding. Can't a guy have a fantasy?" Then he took Victoria in his arms and kissed her with such passion that she almost fell back, but he was there to catch her as she melted into his arms.

"Maybe we should wait."

"Good idea." He laughed as he released the button.

"What about Morgan? Is he home tonight?"

"Nope. Guess where he is."

"I don't know."

"I'll give you a clue. He's with, in his words, 'a wonderfully sexy, beautiful woman.' He's with none other than your mother."

"Really? I guess I'm missing everything that's going on in my house, but that makes sense. She has been a little quiet these days. She usually has something to say about everything, but now she keeps herself busy. She's even exercising, which she's always hated. And she's also cooking special meals, recipes she's never made before. Is Morgan a good cook?"

"The best."

"Well, now I know why the house smells so good. I just assumed my mother was bored and trying new things, but I guess there's something more exciting than just cooking going on. I wonder if Morgan has met the neighborhood grandparents she feeds every day."

"Apparently, Morgan is in love for the first time in his life. And he says they have a great time with your mom's daytime friends, eating and playing cards."

"You know about that?"

"I sure do. Morgan seems very happy with his new friends. As far as I know, he didn't have many friends before. Or if he did, he never mentioned them."

Victoria didn't say much after that. What could she say? There she was, sneaking around and trying to keep her marriage to Jack a secret. She wasn't acting like the adult in the family.

Her kids deserved to know the truth, but somehow she was afraid that they wouldn't understand. After her divorce from Michael was final, Victoria had made a promise to never let anything stand between her kids and their future—and then she met a man and married him just like that. She had to talk to her kids before she could relax into her new marriage.

Jack was also doing some soul searching. He loved their time together, when it was just the two of them, but he wasn't even sure if her dog liked him—not to mention her children, who would probably think of him as a threat to their mother's love. Still, in his opinion, he and Victoria should be adults and tell everyone. He knew family secrets were never good, and things rarely turned out well when people found out.

Could he love her children? And would they love him back? After all, their father was still alive and they loved him. Maybe Michael would have to take some responsibility and the weight of the family would be taken off Victoria. From where Jack stood, it looked like Victoria was the financial backbone of a lot of people. Everyone always counted on her to be a good mother, daughter, sister, and, of course, doctor. Michael was the one who had failed.

That was Jack's assessment, but he didn't think it was fair of him to make an evaluation when he wasn't part of the family dynamic from the beginning. He had started to realize everything he had been telling his patients during therapy might not be that easy to accomplish. He had kept himself arm's length away from getting too close to anyone because he was scared, just like his patients.

• • •

When they got into Jack's penthouse apartment, Victoria saw she was right about Jack's place—everything was perfect, right out of a magazine. She loved what she was walking into. Jack had decorated his entire apartment with white lilies and red roses, and it smelled wonderful. Everything was breathtaking.

What she didn't expect was to find a rabbi waiting for her. Ava was there too, to serve as the witness.

Ava ran over to Victoria and gave her a hug. "I love you for everything you have done for me, and please just know I would never have done anything to hurt you. Michael was there, and I knew there was no way in hell you were ever going to take him back, so I decided to make a move."

Victoria's eyes teared up, and she hugged her sister back. "I love you too. And I do know that. I really do want the best for you, and you're probably right—you might very well be the one to make Michael change. I couldn't help him when we were married, and certainly can't help him now."

After their tearful but joyous reunion, both Ava and Victoria were relieved their feud was behind them. Jack was happy to see he had done the right thing. It could have gone badly, so now he could relax and focus on the rest of his plan.

"Jack, when did you do all of this?" Victoria was so touched by his efforts.

"Today. I was praying you wouldn't change your mind about coming over." Jack looked at the rabbi and Ava with a sense of relief. "Rabbi, do you think it would be okay if we had a few minutes alone before the ceremony? There's something I want to tell Victoria before we celebrate."

"Go ahead," Ava said, as she motioned for the rabbi to have a seat on the couch. "I can keep the rabbi company. I think I need a few prayers while we're at it."

Jack led Victoria into his study, which had floral bouquets throughout the room and expensive chocolates covering the table. Victoria couldn't believe how sweet and wonderful all of this attention was. This whole day was so romantic, she could barely breathe. No one had ever made her feel as much like a woman as Jack did. He seemed to know what she needed when she needed it.

"I have a confession to make," Jack said, taking her hand. "From the moment I ran into you at the book signing, I had a tingling in the pit of my stomach. I started to wonder about if I had gotten your number when we met in college, and how my life might have changed. Did you ever think of me in that way?"

"I have a confession too. When I looked into your eyes that day on Michigan Avenue, I knew I had to see you again. I felt something so familiar in your smile. I knew there was nothing I could do that day, but as soon as I got home that night, I ordered all of your books on my Kindle. When I saw you on the plane, my heart dropped. And when you sat down next to me, I had never felt anything like that before. I couldn't wait to kiss you. I guess it was lucky you were going to the convention."

"That's the other thing. I wasn't, but when I found out you were going to be a speaker, there was no way in hell I wasn't going to be there. And boy, am I glad I didn't talk myself out of going. I was a little afraid to let my guard down, which is probably the reason I never got married. Sometimes fear gets in the way of happiness. That's the doctor in me talking."

"I get it. I know all about fear. I never expected to be in love again. I guess we can't always know the future."

"You're right, and that's a good thing. What do you say we start our life the right way?"

Victoria smiled in approval. "Let's do this."

"Before we do, I have something to ask you." He knelt down on one knee. "Will you be my wife, in sickness and in health, till death do us part?"

"You bet. I'm honored."

Jack opened the small box he was holding and slipped a beautiful, ten-karat diamond ring onto Victoria's finger. They kissed, and that kiss meant something very different than any of the others. It was about love and commitment, all the promises they would keep, and how their respect for each other would be everything they both wanted and would ever need.

When the ceremony was over—after everyone had shared a toast and Ava and the rabbi left—Victoria decided to take a bath to rejuvenate herself after a surreal day. She was so grateful for Jack's decision to have Ava there with her. She hated being at odds with her sister, and she hoped that was the fresh start the two of them needed. Even though they had many disagreements, there wasn't anyone she would have rather had with her to celebrate her new life.

As she closed her eyes, she tried to remember the day she met Jack back in school. She was so naïve at that time. All she ever wanted was to be a doctor, and all these years later, she loved her patients and finally loved her life. Jack was her soulmate, and she wasn't going to lose him, no matter what. She smiled, thinking about Jack waiting for her in bed. Everything seemed to be falling into place.

Then the other shoe dropped. Her phone rang, even though she wasn't on call. After the sixth ring, she finally had to answer.

"You need to come to Northwestern Hospital right now." It was her mother on the phone, and she was upset. "It's Michael. He fell off the roof. The kids are here, and so is Ava. Thank goodness she had just come home. The paramedics came, and before I knew it, he was in the ambulance. This all happened so fast, I couldn't call you until now."

"The roof? What the hell was he doing on the roof at this time of night?"

"Cleaning the gutters," her mother said. "I told him not to, but you know Michael. He rarely listens to anyone. At least he fell on the grass."

"That's comforting. I'll be right there."

"Good. Morgan is on his way to Jack's to get you. He'll bring you here."

When the phone went dead, Victoria couldn't help but wonder how her mother knew she was at Jack's.

• • •

Victoria ran into the emergency room and was greeted by her mother. "You can go talk to Michael," Grace told her. "They just moved him to a room."

"Why was he really at the house?" Victoria asked. "I thought he went away for a while. Just tell me the truth."

117

"He wanted to see the kids, and he accepted my dinner invitation."

"Your dinner invitation? Am I missing something here?"

"I'm quite sure you know about Ava and Michael."

"You know?"

"Not until this happened. When they checked him in, they asked if he was married, and he answered that your sister is his new wife. How quaint. You knew, right?"

Victoria nodded. "I knew, and I'm so sorry you had to find out that way."

"Really? Who keeps secrets like this?"

Victoria looked at her mother, eye to eye. "You! What's with you and Morgan?"

"What about you and Jack?"

"Can we talk about all this later?"

"Michael's waiting for you," Grace continued. "I might add that the kids also heard the answer to the marriage question. Right after that, Ava took them downstairs to get something to eat, and to explain everything. I thought I'd wait for you, so I could hear your version of your productive trip to Vegas. And, don't let me forget, your marriage to Jack."

"So she told you?"

"No she didn't. I already knew."

"That's why you knew where to send Morgan?"

Grace nodded and smiled. "You know, you could have told me. I'm your mother."

Victoria just sat there and didn't say a word. She was trying to figure out how to explain what had happened, but she didn't even want to try. At least not then. She wanted to go to Michael's room, so she could have some time alone with him to talk about the kids. Then her pager rang.

"This can wait until later," Victoria said. "Okay?"

Grace didn't have a choice, so she just nodded that she understood. She knew her daughter usually did the right thing, so she hoped she wouldn't be disappointed after Victoria explained everything. "By the way, he's in room 336."

"Thanks," Victoria called back, as she hopped in the elevator.

When she got upstairs, Maggie, the nurse who had paged her, waved her over. "Hon, now I can see why you got rid of him."

Victoria kissed her hello. "Is he driving you crazy?"

"You've got that right. He's been here less than an hour, and we've been in his room so many times I've lost count. We've got him for the night. Thank God my shift is done in a few minutes."

"How is he?"

"Let's just say he's better than most. Broken legs heal."

Victoria was glad she had kept Michael on her insurance. She knew he wouldn't think it was important enough to get a policy, so she continued to pay his premium. She went to Michael's room and sat down next to him. "Okay, so what did Ava tell the kids?"

"The truth. They were okay with everything. I think the less we talk about this, the better it will be for the kids."

"I'm not so sure," Victoria admitted. "They're just kids, and it's a lot to handle."

"But they're our kids. The divorce was tough, but now, I don't know. We'll be better parents if we're happy."

"Well, we'll see. I hope you're right."

When they all brought Michael home later that night, everyone was too tired to talk, especially the kids. Andrew fell asleep in the car, and Victoria had to carry him in—which was great, because he was usually the one who asked too many questions. Victoria didn't have all the answers, at least not until she had few minutes alone to organize her thoughts.

• • •

Victoria left early in the morning, leaving a note that she had an early meeting. Her thoughts were chaotic, and she knew she had to get all her eggs together before the basket broke and she would have a big mess to clean up.

Two days later, Michael moved into the room off the kitchen. Victoria couldn't say no, because Michael walking up several flights of stairs was certainly out of the question. He had a cast on his right leg and three sets of stiches—one on his forehead, one on his left thigh, and the other on his ankle. That made his mobility very difficult. On the way down from the roof, he fell right into the rosebed that he had planted before they got divorced.

Michael's first night back in his old house was a bit strange, but after three great meals and several snacks, he felt happy to be back. He certainly didn't miss his apartment, where he didn't have a stocked refrigerator or anything else that made it feel like home. He had missed his old house, and the family inside.

Of course, it was a lot different being the ex, but Michael planned to take advantage of every minute he didn't have to go home. Victoria kept her distance, but Grace actually agreed to do his laundry, and Ava was in charge of everything else. He was a happy man in a bad situation.

Angus parked himself on the floor next to Michael's bed. When everyone left the room, Angus jumped up on the bed, licked Michael's face a few times, and then just stared at him.

"I missed you, Angus," Michael said as he lovingly scratched his fur. After the divorce, Angus was certain Michael wasn't coming back. The fact that he did, even if only for a while, made the dog happy.

Michael knew one problem for any divorced couple was someone always got the dog, and in their case, Victoria got Angus. He belonged with the kids, and Michael knew that, but he wished he had gotten custody of him. Angus really was his best friend.

He had wondered many times about why he let every-thing go so easily—his wife, his kids, and everything he used to think mattered. He keep reminding himself that he lost so much money playing cards and going to the track that he had nearly ruined everything that Victoria had worked so hard to attain. He thought he was having fun, but it was no one's fault but his. Being back in his old home made him evaluate everything that he did wrong, making him sad and ridden with guilt—something that tended to come with his Jewish heritage.

"I made a mess of my life, didn't I?" Michael asked, knowing that everyone, including Angus, knew the answer.

"You certainly did, boss." Angus always called him that.

"Well, my friend, it's not over yet. I have Ava."

"Yes, you do. You know she's a handful, don't you?"

Michael knew that, but Angus wanted to remind him of just how difficult things might get. Angus then pranced out of his room, thinking that living in that house required a rest every now and then. Angus needed a private nap, so he disappeared for a few hours. There was so much going on that he wouldn't be missed.

• • •

The next morning, Victoria finally made it to her office. Jessie, the office manager, took one look at her and asked, "So when's the baby due?"

As soon as she said that, Victoria started to cry. She had felt different the last few days, and had wondered if she might be pregnant again. She had just found out for sure that morning.

Jessie escorted her into the coffee room and made sure they were the only ones there.

"So what did Michael say when you told him about the baby?"

"I haven't told him because he's not the father."

Jessie said nothing, but she jumped up, opened the cabinet, and took out a huge chocolate bar. "Join me?"

Wiping her tears away, Victoria reached for some chocolate with a sigh of relief. She didn't stop eating until they had polished off the entire bar, and then she was ready to talk.

They had a long, in-depth conversation, and Jessie comforted her as she always did. It wasn't easy to explain Jack and their relationship, but talking about him reinforced to Victoria that she had made the right decision.

Jessie had been with Victoria since she started her practice, and was still her best friend after all these years. She knew when to talk and when to listen. Jessie was a lot older and wiser, and Victoria always felt lucky to have her as a confidant. She also kept the office on schedule and intact every day, without exception.

"How did you know?" Victoria couldn't help but ask.

"You have two different shoes on. You do that when you're pregnant."

"I do?" Victoria looked down at her feet. Sure enough, she was wearing one black shoe and one navy shoe.

"In all three of you pregnancies, you had several different-shoe days."

"And you didn't tell me?"

"No. It was kind of cute."

Victoria still wasn't sure when it would be the right time to tell her kids about Jack, but it would have to be soon.

As Victoria was finishing up her paperwork, and her office was finally clear of patients, Jessie called out to her. "It's the hospital. It's Johnny. His parents are waiting for you. It's not good."

"Tell them I'm on way, and I'll call the hospital from the car."

Fortunately, Victoria's practice mostly saw well babies and schoolkids with sore throats, coughs, and the usual childhood ailments. But every now and then, when she had a very sick child, she spent a lot of time with their families. Nothing was harder than having to watch parents saying goodbye to their child, and Victoria certainly couldn't let them be alone. Just knowing she was there for them might help in some small way.

After she signed in at the hospital, Victoria stood outside of Johnny's room, taking a few deep breaths to energize herself. When she peeked in, Johnny was alone. She knew his parents had been there by the coffee cups and half-empty plates of leftover food. Marie and Robert were wonderful people with a sense of who they were.

They didn't have a lot of money, but they had love, which was all Johnny needed at the moment.

Victoria walked closer to the bed and sat down. She held Johnny's hand and closed her eyes, praying for an easy death. They had tried everything possible, and still the cancer spread. Victoria patted his head, kissed his cheek, and left with an empty feeling in her heart. When he came to her as an eight-year-old patient with multiple cancers, he was already very ill and unresponsive to treatment. She found him a great oncologist who put him on a new drug, and he had a three-year remission. After that remission, however, it was one bad day after the next.

She walked down to the chapel and saw both of his parents kneeling down and praying, a frequent activity for them. She didn't want to interrupt, so she sat behind them, closed her eyes, and prayed. At that moment, it didn't matter what religion they believed in—they were all one.

Johnny's mother turned back to her and smiled. She got up and took Victoria's hand. "Thank you, Doctor Victoria," Marie said. "You did everything for my little boy. Thank you for the extra time we had. It was beautiful."

They hugged for a moment, and then Marie went back to her son's room. Her husband followed her lead. It appeared that his strength came from his wife. When they got to the room, there was just enough time for them to say goodbye before their little boy closed his eyes forever.

Victoria stood outside and cried. It was never easy losing a patient. No matter how many times it happened, it always felt like the first time. Somehow, this death seemed to really penetrate her soul.

She started questioning everything she had done in the last few weeks. She had never lied to her kids or her family before, and every day that she harbored her secret was one more day she shouldn't.

Chapter Fifteen

Three days later, at an informal family dinner, Victoria made the decision to tell everyone about her marriage. She wasn't going to talk about the baby—at least not yet.

She hadn't even told Jack, because she was waiting for the right time. In truth, she was afraid he might not want any more children. He probably assumed she wouldn't either, figuring three was more than enough.

Victoria tapped her spoon on the water glass she was holding, looking directly at Jack—not at Grace, or Morgan, or her kids, or her seemingly permanent house-guests, Michael and Ava. Victoria was positive Michael had asked his doctor to keep the cast on for a few weeks longer than necessary just so he could continue to live there.

"Okay, here you go," she began. "You know I love all of you, including Angus, the best little friend anyone could have." That was enough for Angus to start moving to a quieter spot.

Andrew stood up and said, "Tell us something we don't know. We know about you and Jack. There isn't too much happening around here that we don't know about." Allyson smiled, and so did Noah.

"You'd be surprised at the info we pick up around here," Noah chimed in. "We're okay as long as you guys are happy. If you're not, we're not. So can we go and play some games before bed? We're all good here."

"And Grammie, we know about you and Morgan," Andrew added. "We like Morgan. He drives a lot better than you do. Sometimes we feel like we're on a horse when you drive. It's such a jumpy ride. Sometimes I feel like throwing up."

Then Grace stood up and tapped her spoon against her water glass. "I guess it's my turn to come clean. I know you all thought there would never be another man in my life, but that was wrong. There were so many days when I would sit by myself and watch TV alone, and I was fine. I had all of you to keep me busy. Then, something wonderful happened, and Morgan came into my life like a flash of light. And now I don't want to be without him, especially at our age. So saying that, Morgan has something to say."

Ava hooted loudly; she couldn't help herself. "Don't tell us you're going to have a baby!" They all laughed, lightening up the conversation.

Morgan smiled as he walked over toward Grace, took her hand, and kissed it. "We got married in Vegas," he said. "This is my bride. Something so wonderful happened to my life when I met Grace. So there you have it. There must have been something in the water we all drank. So, as Jack's mother Sophie would say, 'Mazel Tov to all of us.' She loves weddings. And for an added surprise, there's a special guest at the door."

Jack knew what was coming next. No wonder his mother cut him short when he called that afternoon.

Sophie entered, looking very rested, and Jack knew why—she had freshened up her face with a new lift, adding to her long list of cosmetic surgeries. Her striking white hair sat softly off to one side, and Jack thought she looked pretty good.

"Mom," he said, as he kissed her hello. "Meet the Hudsons and the Feingolds."

Sophie's new boyfriend, George—or "Georgie Baby," as she called him—paraded in after her. Then, she asked the question she'd always anticipated. "Well, which one of you is my new daughter?"

Victoria raised her hand. "That would be me."

Sophie would be there for only one night. Grace was happy about that, because Jack's mother didn't stop talking from the minute she said hello. Whatever the subject, Sophie had something to say about it. Grace usually spoke up, but this was a short visit, and she would be the bigger person. Even Georgie didn't get a word in edgewise.

Jack left early in the morning, and Victoria left even earlier. It appeared that everyone had somewhere to go that Saturday. Even Angus was nowhere to be found.

Chapter Sixteen

It appeared that the kids handled the news about all three marriages very well. Leave it to kids to understand and put things in the right perspective. It was surprising to Victoria, but not to Grace—she and the kids always talked about real life when they were together.

Grace knew that her grandchildren liked hearing the truth, and that was what everyone needed at the end of day. She was sorry she didn't tell the kids sooner. The last few months were chaotic, but also some of the best days she had ever had.

After dinner, and after all the presents that Sophie brought were opened, Morgan and Jack went out to the patio for a smoke. Jack didn't actually smoke, but Morgan had a cigar every now and then. Jack usually held a cigar too, making Morgan feel the informality of a great conversation between a father and son. Morgan loved that about their relationship—Jack was always respectful, and Morgan was appreciative, a wonderful blend of friendship.

"Morgan, my man, how does it feel to find the woman of your dreams?"

"Doc, let me tell you. The minute I walked into this house, I knew Grace was someone I had to know better. I'm in love, and it feels damn good." Morgan smiled as he puffed away. "And you? I was beginning to think you never would, and that would have been a damn shame. You could have ended up like me, letting too many years go by without love. Is Victoria what you always wanted?"

"Truth be told, no. She's what I always needed, but I didn't realize it before. I had seen her once before in college, but I never knew her name. Even then, I would sometimes see her face when I closed my eyes at night. When I saw her outside Maxwell Meyers, I remembered her like it was yesterday. She hadn't changed at all. I was going to be sure that she wasn't getting away this time."

Morgan smirked. "Boss, looks like we both got it right."

"Yes, we did. Now all we have to do is move in here, and we'll be one happy family. I think. That verdict is still out."

Morgan laughed. "You're kidding, right?"

"I don't know, but we can call this place our home for now. Also, before I forget, we need to get a new coffee machine. Believe it or not, they don't have a coffeemaker that makes espresso here."

"This is going to be quite an experience. You don't have all the luxuries you're used to. Is this going to be a deal breaker?"

For the first time ever, Jack lit the cigar and puffed a few times. "Let's just take it slow while I look for a bigger house. I just didn't want to upset Victoria. I think she loves it here."

"Actually, they all seem to," Morgan added. "Maybe this is the piece of the puzzle we've been missing. Her ex seems to be happy as a lark here. He seems to be taking his sweet time getting better, and no one seems to notice he keeps canceling his therapy appointments."

"Well then, we're going to have to make sure he gets better fast!"

Morgan laughed. "Got it. Guess I should stop taking him to Al's Beef. He loves those beef sandwiches and fries."

"Might be a good way to start. Have you overheard him cancelling?"

"Yes and no. He tells everyone when we're out that he's been to therapy. I'll make it my priority to say no. I just felt sorry for the guy. He seems lost, but he does know how to lie very well. I'll give him that."

• • •

Everything was now out in the open, and it was time to make everything more permanent. Victoria and Grace went to help Jack and Morgan pack a few things. There was plenty of room in Victoria's house for all of them. It was a little bit overwhelming for Jack, because he was used to quiet and everything in its place. His apartment looked like the "after" photo in a magazine makeover spread; Victoria's home was the "before."

Victoria had faith that they could all live there happily ever after, but Grace knew that was definitely not going to happen. Victoria had a way of finding the good in everything, while Grace faced the music.

Packing was not easy, because this was a new venture for all of them. Jack wasn't entirely comfortable having Victoria pick and choose what he needed, while Morgan seemed delighted to have someone take care of him for a change.

When they got home, the house was quiet. Ava had always been able to handle her niece and nephews—who were now her stepchildren. And if that wasn't confusing enough, she had just found out she was having a baby. She hadn't told Michael, but she would. They weren't planning to stay at Victoria's once Michael got better, but the food was great and their laundry was done. Ava didn't have to clean anymore, and now that Morgan appeared on the scene, she didn't even have to make coffee. It was going to be hard to leave, but things would be a little too crowded with a baby coming.

Victoria and Jack were able to fall asleep as soon as they got home. They were both exhausted. A few minutes after Jack's eyes closed, he felt something furry in his face. He got up and looked directly into Angus's eyes. At first he was too shocked to say anything, so Jack closed his eyes, hoping he was dreaming. He wasn't, because a couple seconds later, Angus was breathing on him.

Victoria sensed Angus was there. "Honey, he probably wants to go out."

So Jack, trying to be worthy of his new life with kids and a dog, put on his robe and waited for Angus to follow—but he didn't. Instead, Angus took his usual place on the bed, and it was then that Jack realized he had taken over Angus's spot.

Now that Jack was up, he wasn't tired anymore. By that time, Victoria got up. When she realized Jack wasn't there, she looked over and saw him sitting on a chair and watching TV. "Can't you sleep?"

"Go back to bed," Jack said. "Don't worry about a thing. You need your rest." In a minute or less, she was out for the count, and Angus was still in his spot.

After a few minutes, Jack tried to lure Angus out of the room, but nothing seemed to be working. He tried talking. "If I'm up, you're up," he said, but still nothing happened. Finally, he had a thought. "How about a nice salami sandwich?"

That did the trick; Angus was ready to go. They didn't have salami, but they did go outside in the backyard. Angus started first. "Jack, we need to talk."

"Okay, what did you want to talk about?" Jack stopped himself, realizing this marriage had made him crazy. He was talking to a dog. "Okay, who else do you talk to?"

"Victoria and Michael."

"Anyone else?"

"Nope, not yet. But I've been here for a while. You need to write yourself a prescription. This is a tough crowd here." Jack nodded, realizing he was perceptive for a dog. Angus lifted his leg ready to go, but then stopped. "Sorry, false alarm. Maybe we should go in."

This time, Jack closed the bedroom door behind him, keeping Angus out. He quietly went back to bed, but couldn't help himself. He woke Victoria.

"Are you okay?" she asked as she sat up.

"This is going to sound crazy. Does Angus talk?"

"He does. He must like you. He doesn't talk to everyone." Then she slowly slipped under the covers and went back to bed.

In the morning, Angus was back in the bed, but this time he was sleeping between them.

• • •

Jack left early, but Victoria had a late day, so she slept through breakfast. Breakfast was when everything was up for grabs, and she was happy to have one day when she could just stay in bed and think.

Her most pressing thought was Michael, and how to get him well and out of the house. Now that he was married to Ava, their departure would be like killing two birds with one stone. Victoria loved her sister, but living with her was a nightmare. Ava knew she was a handful, but her mother never stopped treating her like a child, so she just kept acting like a spoiled one. Victoria figured Ava and Michael were a match made in hell, but she hoped they would stay married forever—and grow up to be adults very soon.

She needed to start the ball rolling, and Michael was easier than Ava. So Victoria knocked on the door to his room, and peeked in when he didn't answer. She didn't see him or anyone there. She should have walked out, but she closed the door behind her and sat down on the bed to think. All of a sudden, Michael came in from the bathroom and stood before her, wearing only a towel. He was moving rather fast, and he wasn't wearing his cast.

"What the hell, Michael?" Victoria said. "Your cast is off?"

Michael just looked at her, and then looked down at his leg. "And so it is."

"How long?"

"Just a week or so."

"What the hell? Does Ava know?"

"Not yet, but I'm pretty sure she's going to know tonight."

"I'm not telling her—you are. She is your wife. Lucky her."

"Can you blame me? I miss the service and food, and the house. And, most of all, you."

"Do you love my sister?"

"Of course I do, but old habits are hard to break."

"Maybe you should think about a job."

Michael sat on the bed next to her. "I have one. I'm going back to teaching."

"Great. When would that be?"

"As soon as I'm better, which I assume will be very soon."

Victoria sat there for a minute. She was mad, but trying to keep her stress level down. Michael had a funny way of making her feel as if her blood pressure was over the top. He was way too needy, and she hoped that her sister could handle him.

"Tell her tonight," Victoria said, "or I will."

"Just for the record, your sister accepts me as I am. She gets me in a way you never did."

Headed for the door, Victoria mumbled to herself. "Funny thing is, we finally agree on something."

That night at dinner, they all celebrated Michael's cast being off, and he walked with the help of a crutch. He found he liked authenticity.

After dinner, Jack took Angus out for a walk. Jack had taken a liking to Angus. He had always wanted a dog when he was a kid, but Sophie used to say, "When you grow up, you can buy yourself a dog." When Jack grew up, however, he didn't.

Now, his life was different, and this was a change he hadn't seen coming. His next book would probably be very different from his others, because he now had a family. A real family.

Angus wasn't talking, and that was fine. Sometimes Jack liked quiet, and he had experienced a lot of commotion since he met Victoria. As Jack headed back to the house, Michael was waiting outside.

Angus decided it was now or never. "Did they throw you out?" he asked Michael.

"No, just getting some air. Mind if I talk to Jack myself?"

Angus was a little disappointed. He always liked to be where the action was, and he was very curious. He knew three was a crowd, but his lips would be sealed.

"Fine, you can stay."

Michael knew he needed to get a few things off his chest, so he could leave and have a fresh start. "Okay, I know what you're thinking. I'm a shit."

"That really wasn't what I was thinking, but go on." Jack was a good listener, part of his profession. He believed in letting people speak their minds.

"Well, whatever you're thinking, I'm a shit. I did some really bad things, and I'm not proud of that. But I'm going to do whatever it takes to have a good life with Ava, even though she's a handful."

Angus couldn't help but add, "You've got that right."

"Michael, I don't want to think badly of you, and I know you feel bad," Jack said. "Sometimes in life, it takes a lot more work for some of us to get to where we need to go. But I think you're going to make it, because you want to. If you need me, I can help—not as a doctor, but as your brother-in-law. We were friends, and our lives went in different directions, but that's okay. Life changes as we're speaking."

They shook hands and walked back into the house. Angus wasn't far behind. "You don't see this in the movies," he said.

Chapter Seventeen

Victoria was feeling pretty good, but she was pushing it if she waited much longer. Jack wasn't stupid. He would sense something was wrong, even though he didn't yet know that much about her. Right then, she was feeling lucky that he didn't.

She hadn't told anyone except Jessie about the baby. So for the time being, her office was her place of refuge, where she could close her door and take a nap. So in a way, it was good that Jessie knew.

Victoria knew a lot of obstetricians, but Dana Flemmings had delivered her three kids, and was a great friend as well as a terrific doctor. When she arrived for her appointment, she noticed her sister was in another room and the door was open.

Ava was sitting on the examining table reading a magazine, with a sheet wrapped around her and her legs dangling off the side. Victoria tried to walk by unnoticed. But just as she thought the coast was clear, Ava called out to her. "Hey Doc, fancy meeting you here. What are you doing here?"

"Just here for my annual checkup. Is everything okay with you?" Victoria asked as she moved in closer.

Ava wasn't one to keep secrets. "Guess what? I'm pregnant."

Victoria smiled, and gave her a short hug. "Does Michael know?"

"Not yet, but I'm sure he will be happy. You know how much he loves his kids."

Victoria smiled as she responded, "Yes, he does."

"Does Jack know about yours?"

"No, not yet." Victoria realized she shouldn't have answered, but it was too late to take it back. Ever since they were little, Ava had always been able to get secrets out of Victoria with a fast, unassuming question. Now that the cat was out of the bag, Victoria would tell Jack that night—just as soon as she figured out how to do it. "Ava, don't tell anyone until I get home. Okay?"

"I was going to ask you the same thing. I know my situation isn't exactly the best for bringing a baby into the world, but maybe it's time Michael actually grew up."

Victoria was thinking the same thing about her. "Jack took the kids for dinner. So tonight might not be the best."

"I bet Morgan went with them."

"Nope, Jack drove himself. He thought he should get to know the kids better."

"Hope it's not someplace fancy. You know how great they do in chic places. They get a little antsy and other patrons aren't that thrilled, but Jack can handle them. That's what he writes about."

"Yes he does, so let's hope the evening goes well. Writing about kids and being with someone else's kids aren't always the same thing."

"But they're your kids."

"Exactly. I wanted to give him time to catch his breath before I tell him about the baby. I hope he doesn't run for the door."

"He loves you. It will be fine."

"Hope so. Thanks for saying that." Victoria now felt much better, and that much closer to her sister. The two of them being pregnant at the same time would be pretty insane, but maybe it would be fun. However, Grace would have her hands full; Ava was a lot needier than Victoria had ever been.

Victoria waved goodbye and went into her assigned room. "See you later."

. . .

That night turned into an event for Jack. He took the kids to a restaurant he loved in the city, which specialized in great steaks. He had never really seen the kids finish their food at home, but thought they might like the food there. That was his first mistake.

When they walked in, everyone was very nice to Jack, because he stopped by for a steak and some great conversation whenever he had time. Jason, the owner, was a longtime friend, and another confirmed bachelor who just got married about a year ago. He and Jack used to frequent clubs together, often competing to see how fast they could leave with a woman. Jack usually won.

Every table was covered with a white tablecloth and had a carafe of ice-cold water with lemon. Once they were seated, it only took a minute before the carafe was on the floor in a million pieces and there was water everywhere. After the servers cleaned up, the kids were amused with their phone games and Jack decided he could take a call. After answering, he realized he should have stayed focused on the kids. Andrew ran to the bathroom, and Jack motioned for Noah to shadow him, just to be sure he didn't wander off.

Jack was deciding what to order, but thought Allyson could help. "So what do you guys want to eat?"

"Mushroom pizza."

"Well, I don't think they have that. They have spaghetti and meatballs."

Allyson turned her nose up. She was now thinking. "Let me see. We like grilled cheese and fries."

"How about chicken?"

Allyson shook her head. She reached for a menu and started to look it over. Then Andrew came running in and accidently ran into a server. It wasn't a pretty picture. Lobster and shrimp were lying on the floor, and a well-done steak turned up on a man's head, knocking off his hairpiece—which his young girlfriend clearly found amusing. He didn't.

Jack motioned for the maître de', and apologetically gave him his credit card. "So sorry. It's on me. The food, the hairpiece, and their check. I'll pay for everything."

Less than five minutes later, they were out of there. Jack and the kids were laughing—somewhere between the time they walked into the restaurant and leaving, a connection happened. Jack got the message loud and clear. They were kids, and he used to be one too.

As soon as the valet service brought his car around and the kids jumped in, he felt a relationship brewing. "So, kids, how about beef sandwiches and fries?"

Andrew shouted out, "Yeah. I'm starved." He and Allyson began to laugh again. "Wasn't that guy's hair so funny? He wasn't too happy, was he?"

Jack wanted to be a grownup and say something exceptionally bright. Instead, he started to laugh. "Okay, seatbelts on and we're off to Al's."

Andrew was happy. "Dad loves Al's."

Jack smiled. "I think I once heard that."

Chapter Eighteen

Victoria and Jack met at his condo for a night alone, a much-needed chance to spend some time together without the family. Victoria got there early, so she decided to take a bath and just lay there in bubbles and relax. Leaning her head back, she closed her eyes, trying to think of a good way to break the news to Jack. Nothing riveting came to mind.

Jack realized that she was in the tub, so he quietly tiptoed into the bathroom, only to find that she had fallen asleep. Instead of waking her, he went back into the living room. He lit the fireplace, turned down the lights, and turned up the music. He closed his eyes as he sat down on the couch, feeling very relaxed. For him, this was a new thing. When he was finished with work or a book signing, he usually went out for a great dinner with a beautiful woman, or went to a club and met one. He now felt so lucky to be with Victoria, and for him there was nothing more special than that.

While he dozed for a short while, Victoria woke up and put on something very comfortable—a lace wrap with nothing on underneath. She hadn't started to show yet, so she still felt sexy. She usually didn't have time to shop, but she wanted to look beautiful. She liked not having to apologize for not having time to look sexy and alluring for her husband.

Jack opened his eyes, staring at his lovely wife bringing him a glass of wine. "I'm so happy to see you," she said as she snuggled next to him.

"What about you?" he asked as he took a sip and kissed her.

"Not tonight. I just want to relax, be with you, and possibly have some chocolate."

Jack laughed as he took out a large bar of chocolate. "I know my wife, don't I?"

"You do get me, don't you?" Then she kissed him, softly and very sweetly. She had never remembered a night like that with Michael. Everything was so different with Jack; he was so kind and so loving. Victoria had never thought she would be in love again, or so completely. She had never imagined her life would be so wonderful.

Just then, Jack changed the music. "I think we should dance. We have never danced together. I want to see how it feels to dance with the woman I love."

"You're right. We haven't."

The music was smooth, and Jack loved dancing. He took Victoria's hand and gently pulled her toward him. Then he took her in his arms and held her closely as they swayed to the music, kissing as they danced.

"Thank you for taking the kids to dinner," Victoria whispered in his ear. "They haven't stopped talking about it. They really like you. And I really love that you took the time to be with them. That means a lot to me."

Jack kissed her again. "They're great kids, and someday maybe we will have one."

Victoria closed her eyes and smiled, realizing that might be the time. "So how soon were you thinking?"

"Don't know," he said as he dipped her.

"Well, is it sooner or later? Could it be sooner?"

Jack stopped dead in his tracks. "Are you saying what I think you're saying?"

She nodded. "We're having a baby."

Jack felt something so powerful, a feeling he couldn't describe. He hadn't known how much he wanted a baby until she told him.

"Jack. Are you okay with this?"

He turned off the music and sat down on the sofa. He opened the chocolate bar and started munching on it. "I am just feeling a little hungry." He surprised himself as he said that. But he really was feeling good about having a baby—so much so that he picked up his phone and called his mother. He was already changing into a family man.

• • •

Another family dinner was planned. Grace loved the dinners when everyone was there, and the family was growing. She was happy that her family had such wonderful surprises.

The kids were fine when they heard the news in private about Jack and Victoria's baby. In fact, they were better than fine, even Andrew. He liked the fact that he would be a big brother.

During dinner, Grace clicked her glass with the spoon. "We have another wonderful announcement tonight. Ava has some news."

Ava was not ready to talk about it, but she didn't seem to have a choice. "Okay, everyone. I got a promotion at work, and a lot more money. Must be my wonderful skills at booking vacations. The travel agency has decided that I should head my own department."

Ava glanced at Victoria, waiting for a remark, but Victoria didn't say a word. She just thought it to herself; some things were better left unsaid. Grace smiled at Victoria, knowing what she was thinking, and very thankful she kept her thoughts private.

Ava wasn't finished. "Michael will be starting his new teaching job next week, and we will probably be leaving to have our own place very soon."

Michael looked happy, and Victoria wanted to stand on the table and do a happy dance. Soon she could have her life back. As much as she loved her sister, she was thrilled to have them both leave. Less friction and stress—who wouldn't want that?

Ava clicked her spoon to the glass. "More news, everyone." She looked at Victoria. "Is it okay?"

Victoria happily nodded. "The floor's all yours."

Angus was in the other room, but came in when he heard the clicking of the spoon. He hated missing announcements.

Ava looked very happy. "Guess who else is having a baby?"

Everyone looked around the room. "This is big," Angus thought to himself.

"Michael and I are having a baby."

Michael was taken completely off guard. "Did I hear you say we're having a baby?"

"Yes you did."

Just as he got up to kiss Ava, he tripped and fell. He didn't hit his head, but he fell directly on his arm. Ava bent down to see if he was okay, but he screamed when she touched his arm. "Wow, that hurts."

Ava looked down. "Is that okay about the baby?"

"It's good. I'm happy, very happy. But Victoria, could you take a look at my arm? I'm not sure I can move it."

Victoria leaned down. "Looks like a break. You need to get an x-ray."

Ava kissed his forehead. "Are you happy about the baby? Really?"

"Damn right I am. Just have a little pain right now."

Andrew repeated, "Damn right he is." Grace gave him a look. "Sorry, Grammie."

Angus started to walk away, but he hesitated for a moment and moved over toward Victoria. "Guess who's not moving out? It's no wonder we call this place Grand Central Station."

Andrew heard that. "Mommy, did you hear Angus talk?"

Victoria nodded. "I did, but let's not tell anyone right now. Sometimes it's okay to have a secret."

Andrew smiled. "Really?"

Angus whispered in his ear. "Really."

Andrew gave Angus a hug. "So are you like my brother now?"

"Maybe," Angus answered, and then walked off to take his nap. It was another one of those long, tough days for the Winstons, Feingolds, and Hudsons.

The End

About the Author

Marsha is a partner of World Of Ink Network radio shows on Blog Talk Radio and the author of six published books and 11 feature-length screen-plays. Her published works include *Love Changes*, a romantic novel about a family in crisis, and *To Life*, a non-fiction biography about being a teenager and surviving the Holocaust. She has also written five books for young children, *Snack Attack*, *The Magical Leaping Lizard Potion*, *I Wish I Was A Brownie*, the children's mystery *No Clues No Shoes*, and the poetry collection, *The Busy Bus*. She has also published a book version of her romantic comedy screenplay, *It's Never Too Late*.

Wanting to help new writers reach their goals, Marsha founded the literary agency Marcus Bryan & Associates in 1996, and achieved signatory status from the Writers Guild of America (WGA) within two years. Continuing with her goals she is the president of Michigan Avenue Media Inc. where she and her staff help writers expand their careers with affordable marketing.

Find Marsha at

www.MarshaCasperCook.com

&

www.WorldOfInkNetwork.com